BURIED TRUTHS

ALICE WALSH

© 2013, Alice Walsh

 Canada Council Conseil des Arts
for the Arts du Canada

Canada

 Newfoundland
Labrador

We gratefully acknowledge the financial support of the Canada Council for the Arts,
the Government of Canada through the Canada Book Fund (CBF),
and the Government of Newfoundland and Labrador through the Department
of Tourism, Culture and Recreation for our publishing program.

All rights reserved. No part of this work covered by the copyrights hereon may
be reproduced or used in any form or by any means—graphic, electronic or
mechanical—without the prior written permission of the publisher. Any requests for
photocopying, recording, taping or information storage and retrieval systems of
any part of this book shall be directed in writing to the Canadian Reprography
Collective, One Yonge Street, Suite 1900, Toronto, Ontario M5E 1E5.

Cover Design by Todd Manning
Layout by Joanne Snook-Hann
Printed on acid-free paper

Published by
TUCKAMORE BOOKS
an imprint of CREATIVE BOOK PUBLISHING
a Transcontinental Inc. associated company
P.O. Box 8660, Stn. A
St. John's, Newfoundland and Labrador A1B 3T7

Printed in Canada by:
Marquis Imprimeur

Library and Archives Canada Cataloguing in Publication

Walsh, Alice (E. Alice)
    Buried truths / Alice Walsh.

ISBN 978-1-77103-009-0

    I. Title.

PS8595.A5847B87 2013   jC813'.54   C2013-900510-2

BURIED TRUTHS

ALICE WALSH

Tuckamore Books
a Creative Publishers imprint

St. John's, Newfoundland and Labrador
2013

For Dennis
And to the memory of our faithful, four-legged friend, Farley

CHAPTER 1: Leaving

"I have no hope that he's undrowned."
William Shakespeare, *The Tempest*

The plane bumped along the runway like an injured bird, a stewardess giving instructions for what to do in case of an emergency. Zoë had never been on a plane before and as it rose steadily into the grey sky, she felt a shiver of excitement and nervousness. As the plane climbed and banked, Toronto tilting beneath her, she peered down into backyards and parking lots. The aircraft climbed higher, cars and trucks shrinking to the size of dinky toys, swimming pools to the size of puddles. Zoë leaned her head against the small oval window, the ache in her chest making it difficult to breathe. Never had she felt so completely abandoned, so totally alone. *I'm being sent away*, she thought. *Sent away to live with strangers. And to Newfoundland, of all places—the tail end of Canada, the end of the earth.*

Turning from the window, she let her gaze fall on the woman beside her. Long red fingernails fluttered over the keys of her laptop like moths. Zoë's mother had never got the hang of typing and dropped out of a business course at the community college. She ended up taking night courses in Early Childhood Development while cleaning houses by day. After she graduated, she got a job at Pop Goes the Weasel day care. The pay wasn't much better than she earned cleaning houses, but Mum loved the job and the little kids she worked with.

Zoë closed her eyes, sadness shrouding her like a thick fog. Had it only been seven months since her whole life was turned upside down? Only seven months since Mr. Pike, the vice-principal, knocked on the door of her French class and spoke quietly to Madame Benoit? Zoë pictured it all in her mind's eye. The teacher stepping out into the hallway, closing the door behind her. The worried look on her face when she returned. The small quiver in her voice when she asked Zoë to gather her things and go with the vice-principal to his office. As Zoë shoved textbooks and notebooks inside her backpack, the class got very quiet. The only sounds were the tinkling of Madame Benoit's bangle bracelets and Brian Dobson tapping his fingers, a habit he had when he was nervous.

In the hallway Mr. Pike had put his hand on Zoë's shoulder; the pity in his eyes was obvious. Heart pounding, she followed him to his office bracing herself for the bad news she knew would come. Aunt Caroline was in the outer office talking with the secretary, her eyes red from crying. When she saw Zoë she broke into fresh tears.

Her memory from that point on was fragmented. She recalled phrases—"your mother," and "stepped in front of traffic" and "killed instantly"—but she couldn't remember exactly how Aunt Caroline delivered the news. She took Zoë home with her that afternoon. Even now, the events seemed unreal and nightmarish.

The funeral was held at the Church of St. Martha where Mum did volunteer work. The church had a food bank and a drop-in centre for the homeless. Zoë sat in the front pew with Uncle Paul, Aunt Caroline, and their daughter, Amber, who was her best friend. Throughout the opening hymns, Zoë kept her head down and wept.

"We are here today to mourn Maureen Martin, whom God has called to her eternal reward," the minister began the service.

Maureen. The name sounded strange to Zoë's ears. To Mum's friends and co-workers, she was Reenie.

"God called her?" came a loud frightened voice from the back. "Did God take the baby?"

Heads whipped around. There were shocked gasps, followed by nervous titters from mourners in pews around them. The minister swallowed a couple of times, looking flustered.

Zoë didn't need to look around to know it was Suzie Quinn who had spoken. Suzie Q, as people called her, lived on the street. When she wasn't locked up in a mental ward on Queen Street, that is. When Suzie went off her meds, she could get agitated and paranoid. At times she could be coherent, but most of the time, she didn't know what was going on around her.

Despite her own pain, Zoë felt a stab of pity. Mum was about the only friend Suzie had; they'd known each other for years. Suzie often referred to Zoë as "the baby." Mum used to visit Suzie in the hospital nearly every Sunday. Sometimes she was so out of it, she couldn't even remember Mum's name, confusing her with some other person. One evening, Suzie was convinced Mum had died. She became so agitated, a nurse called Mum to come in. It took hours to get her settled down. Mum stopped going to see her after that. "It's just too depressing," she told Zoë. "And I don't think I'm doing her any good."

On the way out of the church, Zoë caught a glimpse of Suzie Q in the foyer, shuffling around, muttering to herself. She was wearing the same heavy coat she wore year round and had various coloured scarves wrapped around her neck. Despite the plastic barrettes, her grey hair stuck out in all directions.

Zoë watched the coffin being loaded into the hearse, her heart breaking. She shivered now, remembering the burial. It was early November. The night before the funeral it had snowed, and a lacy pattern covered the ground, capping the headstones and the fence around the cemetery. The fresh grave with a mound of black earth beside it looked like an ugly wound. As she watched the grey coffin disappear into the deep earth, reality hit hard: she was an orphan now, alone in the world.

People stopped to hug her and to offer condolences. They told her what a great person her mother had been. How much they were going to miss her. Most of the mourners were Mum's friends and co-workers. Some of Zoë's teachers and friends from school came as well.

What followed was a haze of numbness, grief, and nightmares. After the funeral Zoë went to live with Aunt Caroline, Uncle Paul, and their five kids. They set up a cot for her in a room with Amber and her younger sister. Although everyone tried to be kind, Zoë only wanted to be left alone. Aunt Caroline brought her trays of food that she refused to eat. Nothing could ease the overwhelming burden of her pain. At times, she felt her grief was more than she could bear.

It was my art that kept me sane during that horrible time, Zoë thought. Whenever the pain got too great, she went to her easel. Sometimes she got distracted for hours, watching images take shape on the canvas. She had lost all interest in school and thought she would lose her last year of junior high. But in the end, she managed to squeak by.

A little more than six months after Zoë moved in, Aunt Caroline and Uncle Paul began arguing. He had lost his job some months ago, and things were not easy for the family. Shortly afterwards, Aunt Caroline came into Zoë's bedroom. Zoë couldn't help noticing the dark shadows under her eyes as she sat down wearily on the bed across from her.

"I have something to tell you," her aunt said, reaching into her shirt pocket for a package of cigarettes. She had stopped smoking years ago, but took it up again after the funeral.

Aunt Caroline lit the cigarette and got up from the bed. Zoë watched silently as she blew plumes of smoke through the open window. A whole minute passed before she spoke. "I've contacted your father," she said abruptly.

Zoë's mouth dropped open.

"I know," Aunt Caroline said grimly. "It was as much a shock for me as it must be for you."

Zoë stared at her.

Aunt Caroline turned from the window and came to sit on the cot beside Zoë. "He wants to get to know you."

"My father's dead."

Aunt Caroline covered Zoë's hands with nicotine stained fingers. Her nails were chewed to the quick. "No, dear. He's alive, and he wants to meet you."

Zoë pulled her hand away. Her father was dead. Mum wouldn't lie. Why would she?

Mum had told her very little about her father. His name was Mike van der Post. They'd met at a university in Nova Scotia.

Mum wrote poetry and wanted to be a social worker. Mike was in pre-med. When she got pregnant, Mike's family was devastated. They were Dutch immigrants who had worked hard to give their children a good education. Mike still had years of medical school in front of him. His mother urged Mum to have an abortion. Mum went to stay at the Home of the Guardian Angel, a maternity home in Halifax. After Zoë was born she left for Toronto and never had contact with the family again. Later, she learned through a friend that Mike had drowned.

"But he's dead!"

Aunt Caroline smashed out her cigarette and fumbled in her package for another. "No, dear, it seems your mother only told you that." She shook her head. "Your father's very much alive and he wants you to go live with him in Newfoundland."

"Newfoundland?"

Aunt Caroline nodded. "Some little fishing village. His wife's an archaeologist. She's doing research, writing a book on some ancient culture that was discovered there in the sixties."

"They want me to come live with them?" Zoë asked skeptically.

Her aunt squinted through a haze of smoke. "It's about time he shared the burden."

Zoë felt as if she'd been slapped. Is that all she was, a burden to be shared? But she had to keep in mind that Aunt Caroline wasn't her real aunt. She'd been Mum's closest friend since Zoë was a baby. In fact, her own daughter, Amber, had become Zoë's best friend; they liked to think of each other as cousins. Mum had no family of her own. *But why would Mum lie to me?* she wondered, feeling betrayed.

Smoke drifted from Aunt Caroline's nostrils. "You have to understand, Zoë, Mike's mother never approved of Reenie."

Zoë nodded. That much was true enough. Mum said she might have married Mike if it wasn't for his mother. How could Aunt Caroline send her to live with a father who'd abandoned her? If he didn't want her as a baby, why would he want her now? Fear tugged at the pit of her stomach, and she struggled to hold back the tears that were threatening to flow.

Aunt Caroline put her arm around Zoë's thin shoulders. "If things don't work out, you can always come back here."

Zoë nodded, although she knew that wasn't true. She was just another mouth to feed, and already there were too many. So what could she do?

"They both have good jobs," Aunt Caroline said. "Your father's an obstetrician." Her voice was muffled, and Zoë knew she was trying hard not to cry. "Not like Uncle Paul. Always the last to be hired and the first to be let go." She reached for another cigarette but found the package empty. "You have a sister too." Aunt Caroline flapped at her pockets in hopes of finding another pack. "Laura. She's twenty months old."

"Are you okay, dear?" The voice stirred Zoë back to the moment. The woman with the laptop was looking at her, concern showing on her wrinkled face.

"I'm fine," she stammered through a blur of tears.

The kindly woman stared at her a moment longer before returning to her laptop.

I'll never be fine, Zoë thought. Nothing could ease the stabbing pain in her heart. She knew she would grieve for her mother for the rest of her life.

Wiping her eyes, she pulled a photograph from her backpack. Her *family*. Mike had sent the photograph from Newfoundland. She had talked with him a number of times since Aunt Caroline broke the news. Her father seemed nice enough. And judging by all the questions he had asked her, she felt he was interested in her life. Zoë told him about school, about her friends. About an art project she was working on. He told her about his work. His wife, Sarah, had taken a sabbatical, he told her. They'd moved from St. John's where Sarah taught archaeology at Memorial University to Port au Choix, population 1,010, a fishing village smack in the middle of nowhere. It seemed to Zoë like the worst place in the world to live. The town wasn't even on the map until someone accidentally dug up a four-thousand-year-old sacred burial ground. Now, apparently, archaeologists from all over the world went there. Mike got a job with Grenfell Regional Health Services, travelling up and down a stretch of coast holding well-women clinics and delivering babies.

Zoë stared hard at the picture. She never got around to asking Mike the tough questions: Where were you during Mum's pregnancy? Why did you abandon me? Maybe when they were face to face they would have that talk. Zoë turned over the picture and read the back like she'd done a dozen times before. *Mike, Sarah, and Laura at fifteen months*. People often remarked how little Zoë resembled her mother. But now as she studied the photograph, she realized she had not inherited her father's looks either. His hair was as blond as hers was dark, and although she couldn't see his eyes, she was certain that beneath the thick glasses, they were not brown like her own. She used to imagine her father as a handsome, dark haired man, nothing like this man in the photograph with

Chiclet-size teeth and thick glasses. Still, she felt a stir of excitement, knowing she would soon meet him. Sarah was what Mum would have called "plain," with her limp brown hair and narrow glasses. She was holding baby Laura who had curly red hair and pale skin. Strangely, Laura didn't look like her parents either.

A trolley squeaked down the narrow aisle, and a smiling stewardess offered Zoë a little container of apple juice and a chocolate chip muffin mummified in plastic. She opened the juice, took a sip, then turned back to the window. A solid bank of dark clouds had encircled the plane. After a few minutes, a microphone crackled to life. Zoë saw that the "fasten your seatbelt" sign had flashed on. "This is your pilot speaking. Winds are gusting up to ninety in some areas. Be prepared for some turbulence ahead."

CHAPTER 2: Arriving

"My dear one, thee, my daughter, who
art ignorant of what thou art."
The Tempest

Despite the turbulence, the plane landed with hardly a bump, and they were gliding safely down the runway. "Welcome to Deer Lake," a stewardess said into a microphone. "The local time is two-thirty, the temperature nineteen with overcast skies. Please keep your seatbelts fastened until the plane is brought to a full stop."

As Zoë walked across the tarmac her heart was racing, and she tried to squelch the anxiety in her stomach. She was so nervous, she was afraid she might throw up. She was about to come face to face with the father she had wondered about her whole life. As she approached the tiny airport, people were waving excitedly, running toward disembarked passengers with outstretched arms. She scanned the faces in the crowd for Mike and Sarah. They were standing by the luggage carousel, looking exactly as they did in the photograph. Sarah was holding Laura who was wearing a T-shirt that said "Daddy's Girl."

Mike moved toward her, awkwardly holding out his hand. "Zoë?" He smiled. "I'm … I'm Mike, and this is Sarah and Laura."

Sarah flashed her a smile as she shifted Laura to her left hip. Zoë felt short stubby fingers grasp her hand. "I'm pleased to finally meet you, Zoë," she said. Laura buried her head in her mother's neck.

"She's shy around strangers," Mike said, somewhat apologetically. He put his hand on Zoë's shoulder. "Let's go find your luggage."

Zoë felt a tug of disappointment. She was not sure what she expected, but whenever she imagined their reunion, it was more than a handshake at the airport.

Suitcases and bags rolled onto the carousel. Zoë saw her own small plaid suitcase trundling toward her. As soon as it was near enough, she reached out and grabbed it, relieved that the brown belt she had tied around it still held it together.

"The rest should follow shortly," Mike said.

"That's all there is."

"That's it?" Sarah sounded surprised. "I guess your aunt will be sending the rest."

Zoë didn't bother to tell her that the suitcase and her backpack contained everything she owned.

Mike took the luggage, and they started down a wide corridor past a gift shop, information booth, and coffee shops.

Outside, he led them to a red minivan parked not far from the entrance. He opened the side door and gestured for Zoë to climb in. Sarah buckled Laura into her infant seat. "I hope the weather in Toronto is better than our Maritime weather," she said.

"It's not too bad." Zoë hated idle chit-chat, especially talk about the weather, but she realized Sarah was only trying to be friendly.

Sarah closed the door and climbed into the passenger seat. Mike got behind the wheel and started the engine.

Zoë had all kinds of unanswered questions for Mike, but she knew they would have to wait. It was impossible to talk from the back seat with Sarah in the front.

"It's a long drive," Sarah said as they pulled away from the airport parking lot. "Two and a half hours."

"Don't they have an airport that's closer?"

"No," Mike said. "Port au Choix is very isolated."

"No movie theatres or department stores," Sarah added. "Not even a Tim Hortons."

Great, thought Zoë. She imagined sitting in her room all summer reading the two books she'd brought with her. Well, at least she had her art. Mike had told her the scenery in northern Newfoundland was fantastic. The smartest thing she ever did was take that painting workshop the community centre put on for inner-city kids. The instructor told her she was good with colour and composition. Zoë loved looking at objects or landscapes and making something new out of what appeared to be just an ordinary lake or building. She enjoyed the workshop so much that the following summer she enrolled in an art appreciation course.

"They do have a great restaurant," Sarah said, breaking into her thoughts. "The Tempest. In fact, your Opa helped get it started."

"Opa?"

Sarah turned to glance at Zoë, smiling at her baffled expression. "Your grandfather," she explained.

Zoë nodded. She knew from conversations with Mike that her grandfather taught drama part-time at a college in Corner

Brook, about a forty minute drive from Deer Lake. He spent his summers near Port au Choix working with a theatre company, Fathom Five.

"It was Sarah who convinced your Opa to come to Newfoundland," Mike said.

Nodding, Sarah turned to look at Zoë. "I took him to Port au Choix on one of my visits there, and he decided he wanted to buy a house nearby."

For the next while, they drove in silence, Zoë gazing out the window at the passing scenery. It was unlike anything she had seen. So different from Toronto. Towering blue mountains loomed in the distance. Cows and horses grazed in grassy fields. Sheep roamed freely along the side of the road. They passed quaint little fishing villages with names like Rocky Harbour, Cow Head, and Sally's Cove. The houses that dotted the shoreline were one and two storeys with weather beaten clapboard siding.

They stopped at a variety store for ice cream cones, which they ate outside at a picnic table. Sarah talked about her research. "Port au Choix is one of the richest archaeology sites in Atlantic Canada," she said. "An archaeologist's paradise. I'm very excited about my research there."

Zoë nodded politely. She was worried about starting a new school. Would she fit in, or would the other kids see her as an outsider? In Ontario, she always had Amber by her side. But she kept her fears to herself.

It was nearly five o'clock when they came to a battered green sign that said Welcome to Port Saunders.

"Almost there now," Mike told her.

Zoë stared out the window. The outport was built on a hill with houses that sloped toward the ocean. There were boats in the harbour, mountains and blue hills in the distance.

"The high school is over there," Sarah said, after a few minutes. She pointed to a white building half hidden by tall fir trees.

A little while later, they pulled into a timbered subdivision with a sign that said: d'Arby Woods. The houses here all looked newly built and more modern, with brick siding and carports.

"Interesting name," Zoe said.

"Yes," said Sarah, "but people around here refer to it as 'the subdivision.'"

"It's about five kilometres to Port au Choix from here," Mike said as he drove the car into a driveway near the end of the street. A tall boy, who looked to be a year or two older than Zoë, stood in one of the driveways with a kitten on his shoulder. He had dark, wavy hair that touched the collar of his shirt.

Sarah waved. "That's Josh," she explained, "one of our babysitters. The kitten is Zing, a runt rejected by the litter. They didn't think it would survive, but thanks to Josh's nurturing, it has thrived."

Mike turned off the engine. "I'll get your luggage," he told Zoë.

Sarah released Laura from her car seat. Zoë followed her up the walkway to the house. Gingerly, she stepped through the door onto a freshly vacuumed carpet. The house smelled of furniture wax and disinfectant. A polished table in the hallway held a crystal vase filled with fresh flowers. There were large sofas, overstuffed chairs, and a brick fireplace with a large mirror over it. Paintings and photographs adorned the walls, and glass and ceramic figurines were displayed on narrow shelves.

"I'll show you to your room," Mike said.

He led Zoë up a thick-carpeted staircase and down a wide hallway with rows of framed photographs on the wall. "In here," he said, leading her into a bedroom that smelled freshly painted. "Kind of small," he said, apologetically.

Zoë looked around the room, at the double bed with the yellow, ruffled spread and matching curtains. There was a bureau, a bookshelf, and a cedar trunk at the foot of her bed. "It's great," she said. She'd never had a room of her own. She usually shared a room with Mum or slept on a sofa in the living room.

"Supper will be served as soon as Sarah gets around to heating up the Chinese food we picked up in Deer Lake." Mike put a hand on Zoë's shoulder. "Make yourself at home."

"Thanks," she said.

Mike left the room, and Zoë went to the window and looked out at the tree-lined street. So different from the places she and Mum had lived that looked out on back alleys. The boy, Josh, was helping a little boy tie his shoelaces. Their house was across the street and two doors down. The kitten was on the ground beside them. She watched as Josh gently picked it up, stroking it with his finger.

When Zoë went downstairs, she saw that the table was set with fancy plates and cutlery, the Chinese food arranged on china platters. Whenever Mum bought Chinese food they ate it out of the cartons, using chopsticks. They ate their meals at a battered coffee table Mum found at a yard sale.

Zoë looked around the sparkling kitchen with a large island in the centre. White cupboards ran from floor to ceiling. The dining room window looked out over the ocean. In the distance she could see an island with a red and white lighthouse perched precariously on a steep cliff. She imagined capturing the scene on canvas. How would it look in the early morning light? In late evening?

The food smelled wonderful, and Zoë realized she was hungry. After they were seated, Mike placed a platter in front of her. "Enjoy, Zoë," he said.

She helped herself to large portions of beef fried rice, sweet and sour chicken, and egg rolls.

"My sister … your Aunt Anneke and her family are eager to meet you, Zoë," Mike said, "They live in Nova Scotia but are coming to visit your grandparents in a week or so."

"Cool." Zoë added chow mien to her plate. She'd never had a real aunt before, at least, not one she knew about. Mum always said family was important.

"Oma and Opa are out of town," Sarah explained.

Zoë assumed Oma was Mike's mother, Ans. She stared at her plate, remembering the things Mum had told her about Ans. She was not looking forward to meeting this woman who had treated her mother so badly.

"They've separated," Mike said sadly. "After thirty-eight years, they're going to file for divorce. They already live in separate houses. Dad has rented a house not far from here. Mom lives at their house in Cape Prosper, about an hour's drive from here." He speared a chicken ball with his fork. "Your Oma is out of town at the moment, attending some art conference."

Zoë's head shot up. Ans was an artist?

"I seriously doubt they'll go through with the divorce." Sarah shook her head. "It's obvious they still care for each other."

Zoë remained silent.

"Your grandmother has illustrated a number of children's books," Sarah said. She got up from the table and came back holding a glossy picture book that she handed to her.

Zoë looked at the title: *The Cat that Came to The Dog Show*, written by Anne Little, illustrated by Ans van der Post. "To my darling Laura," was written on the title page.

The story was about a cat who fooled everyone into believing she was a dog so she could win a ribbon at a dog show. It was such a funny story that Zoë laughed in spite of everything. *The artwork is quite good*, Zoë thought grudgingly.

Mike smiled at her. "You'll love your grandparents once you get to know them."

Zoë didn't comment. She concentrated on cracking open a fortune cookie and retrieving a tiny ribbon of paper. She read and reread the neatly typed words. *Do not be deceived; things are not always as they appear.*

CHAPTER 3: Port au Choix

"The folly of this island."
The Tempest

Zoë lay awake on crisp blue sheets, the events of the day tossing in her mind. *Mike is a good person*, she decided, *and Sarah seems nice*. Yet despite this, she tossed and turned, unable to sleep. Why had Mum kept her from her father? Was it because of Ans? She flipped onto her stomach, then onto her side, trying to find a comfortable position. Drawing her knees up to her chin, she wrapped her arms around her legs. She often slept this way, a habit that came from living in places with not enough heat.

After a while, Zoë gave up trying to sleep, got out of bed, and switched on the light. Before she left Toronto, Aunt Caroline gave her a couple of Mum's journals she had found while cleaning out the apartment. Whenever they moved—which was often—Mum left things at Aunt Caroline's house. "There's more in the basement," her aunt had told her. "I'll mail them when I can."

Zoë flipped through the pages, admiring the elegant handwriting, the graceful decorative letters. The Cs curled like sculptured waves, the Ms and Ws like winged birds ready to fly off the page. The Ss were as ornate as musical notes. During her stay at the maternity home, Mum had taken a course in calligraphy. Zoë turned to the last entry: November 4, 1996, the day before her mother died. "Zoë is getting older now, and I feel she should know the truth. Dear God, will she hate me for what I have done?"

Zoë stared at the flamboyant script. Did her mother mean keeping her away from Mike? Telling her he was dead when she knew all along he was alive? *Mum, why? Why would you do that to me?* Mum had even led Aunt Caroline to believe Mike was dead. Caroline was flabbergasted when she contacted Mike's parents to inform them of Reenie's death and found out Mike was still alive. Zoë closed the journal. Her mother's behaviour made no sense at all. She would talk this over with Mike when she had the chance.

When Zoë went downstairs for breakfast, a woman was feeding Laura from her highchair. She looked to be in her early sixties, scrawny and wrinkled. Her grey hair was tightly curled, her thin lips smeared with bright red lipstick.

"Oh there you are," she said, glancing up from the bowl of cereal she was spooning into Laura's mouth. "Sleep well, my love?" She had an odd accent. In a way, it reminded her of Mr. O'Connor, Zoë's math teacher, who had emigrated from Ireland.

Zoë stared at her.

"I'm Dora," the woman said. "I looks after little Laura while her mom works."

"Do you live around here?" Zoë asked, feeling she should say something.

"I lives in Port au Choix, my love. Henry drops me off on his way to work."

She didn't explain who Henry was, and Zoë didn't ask.

"Can I get yeh some breakfast? Some eggs and bacon?"

"No thanks," Zoë said. "I'm just going to have toast." She went to the breadbox and took out two slices of bread. Only after she had dropped them in the toaster did she realize that maybe she should have asked first. She was so used to taking care of herself that fixing her own breakfast came as naturally as breathing.

"Sure, you got no accent a'tall," Dora said suddenly.

"Accent?"

"My dear, some people that comes here from the mainland, yeh can't understand a word they says."

Zoë didn't know what to say, so she said nothing.

"There's tea steeping on the back of the stove," Dora said.

Sarah came bustling into the kitchen. "Good morning, Zoë," she said. "I see you've met Dora."

Dora glanced out the window at the dark sky. "Looks like a wet one out there."

Sarah made a face. "It's miserable when it rains. It gets so muddy in the trenches. Last Friday it got so bad, the team had to go home."

"How long will they keep working?" Dora asked.

Sarah shrugged. "Late September, early October."

"Do you find much stuff?" Zoë asked. The toast popped up and she took it out of the toaster and put it on a plate.

"We always find interesting things," Sarah said. "Of course, I don't do a lot of digging.

But I have an agreement with the university that while I'm on sabbatical, I will supervise the sites at times." Laura threw her sippy cup on the floor and Sarah picked it up. "There's a treasure trove of artifacts in the area."

Dora nodded. "Sure, every time a new building goes up, they finds bones or artifacts that belonged to the Maritime Archaic Indians or some other group that lived around here."

"Dora's right," Sarah agreed. "It's amazing."

"Corey called me t'other day," Dora said. "Found some bones while they was digging out the basement for his new house. 'Aunt Dora,' he says. 'Can ye imagine now the problems this is gonna cause me. I feels like chucking them over the fence.'" Dora shook her head. "'Don't yeh dare,' I told him. 'Make sure you reports it.'"

"It's not unusual for people to disturb artifacts when they go to put up a new building," Sarah said. "Once they report it, the work gets held up."

Dora nodded. "And poor Corey's trying to get his basement finished before winter." She turned her attention to Laura. "Done, my love?" She wiped the little girl's face with a cloth before lifting her out of the chair.

Zoë had buttered her toast and poured herself a cup of tea. She took a seat at the kitchen table.

"Sure, I remembers the day they dug up the Maritime Archaic Indians," Dora said. "Back in 1967, it was. Thirty years ago. Same year me and Henry got married. Both of us was working in the fish plant at the time. Right across from the burial site. I was on me break, having a smoke by the wharf when someone told me that T'dore dug up some skeletons with the tractor."

Dora told the story with the relish of someone who had recited it many times before. "We went up to check and sure enough, they had two skeletons uncovered." Her eyes darted from Zoë to Sarah. "And by God, that afternoon didn't they dig up eight more." Dora wiped off the highchair and put the cereal bowl in the sink. "People come here in droves after that. And they're still coming." She shook her head. "We hardly got *any* visitors before then." She laughed. "Except for the few seagulls that flew off course."

I bet they didn't even stay, Zoë thought.

Sarah was nodding and smiling as if she'd heard the story many times. "So much rich history. Right beneath our feet."

"Sounds exciting," Zoë said. It didn't really. In fact, she found the whole conversation boring. Why would people get excited over some old bones?

"Why don't you come to the site with me this morning?" Sarah said.

"Well, gee …" Zoë could have kicked herself for her faked enthusiasm. The last thing she wanted was to watch Sarah dig. She struggled to come up with an excuse.

"Jimmy's working there for the summer," Dora said.

"Dora's son," Sarah explained. "He's studying archaeology at Memorial University. One of my most gifted students."

"We spent thousands of dollars for him to get an education." Dora laughed. "His dad's not too happy that he's back home diggin' holes in the ground."

Sarah went to the closet and came back with a pair of rubber boots and a yellow raincoat. "These should fit," she said, handing them to Zoë.

She groaned inwardly but finished her toast and gulped down her tea.

It was raining a cold drizzle when they left the house and so foggy they could barely see what was in front of them.

"You'll love it," Sarah said. "We're always finding something new and exciting."

After a few minutes, they drove past a battered sign that said: Welcome to the town of Port au Choix, Fishing Capital of Western Newfoundland. "I need to check with the team here," Sarah said as she turned onto a road with a sign that said: Pointe Riche. "This was the boundary line in the French-English fishing dispute in the eighteenth century," Sarah said, sounding like a tour guide. "It's also the site where they discovered the Dorset Paleoeskimo and Groswater Paleoeskimo."

Zoë swallowed a yawn.

Sarah drove past a small lighthouse on an outcrop of rock until she came to an area with shallow trenches roped off with white twine. A number of men and women wearing yellow and black raincoats were busy digging.

"I'll only be a minute," Sarah said. She stopped the car and got out.

The workers were so involved with their work they didn't even look up as Sarah approached. Operating slowly and carefully, they were removing soil with trowels and small brushes. Sarah spoke briefly with a young man before returning to the car.

The second site was in the woods. Sarah drove down a narrow rutted road, branches scraping against the windshield. Rain dripped down from the trees.

No sooner had they stopped the car and got out than a young woman came running toward them. "Dr. Porter," she called excitedly. "Look what we found."

Geez, Zoë thought. *What is it? The Holy Grail?*

Sarah removed her gloves and examined the object carefully. "Looks like a scraper. Used for dressing and preparing hides," she explained. "This one's different from most of the others. Where did you find it?"

"It was in Abbey's pit."

Sarah turned to Zoë. "Alexis, this is my ... Mike's daughter, Zoë. Alexis is one of the site supervisors."

Alexis removed her glove and reached for Zoë's hand. "Pleased to meet you," she said.

"Come meet Abbey," Sarah said. "She lives in our subdivision. She's about your age. I think she's going into tenth grade as well."

Zoë brightened at the thought of meeting someone her own age. She was missing Amber. "She works *here*?"

Sarah nodded. "We hire archaeology students and high school students who have an interest in archaeology."

Why would anyone *have an interest in this kind of work?* Zoë wondered as she followed Sarah to a trench at the far end of the site.

"The school gives students extra credits for working here," Sarah said. "Once Abbey starts school, she will work every other Saturday and get Friday afternoons off from school."

"Hmm." *That might make it worthwhile.*

"The pay is not much," Sarah said, "but it will give you valuable experience."

I could use the money, Zoë thought.

"Got a visitor," Sarah announced as they approached the pit.

Abbey climbed out of the trench and placed her tools carefully on the ground. She took off her glasses and wiped them on her sleeve. "I'm so pleased to meet you," she told Zoë after Sarah had introduced them. She smiled, showing a jumble of crooked teeth. Tendrils of blonde curls escaped from the hood of her rain jacket.

"You work here," Zoë said unnecessarily.

Abbey beamed. "Isn't it exciting?"

You've got to be kidding.

"You could work here too, Zoë," Abbey told her. "Right now we're searching for the Maritime Archaic habitation site. We have no clue where it is, and we're digging trenches all over Port au Choix. That is," she amended, "in places we believe they may have lived."

Zoë looked from Abbey to Sarah, not fully understanding.

"For thirteen seasons, since 1984, archaeologists have been trying to solve the great mystery of where the Maritime Archaic Indians had their habitation site," Sarah explained. "We're all hoping 1997 might be the year it is finally solved."

A woman with long greying hair and clutching a clipboard emerged from out of the woods. Sarah waved as the woman neared them. "Hey Patty," she said, "this is Zoë, Mike's daughter. She's interested in working here."

Whoa, Zoë thought. *That's pushing it.*

"You want to dig?"

"I … I'll think about it."

"Good. Good," Patty said as if Zoë had already made up her mind. "The more people we have digging, the greater the chance of finding a dwelling structure."

What exactly are they looking for? Zoë wondered. She couldn't imagine a house—whether it was a tent or a wooden structure— lasting for thousands of years.

"We are hoping to find evidence of everyday life," Patty said, as if reading her thoughts. "Middens or other activity areas."

"A garbage heap," Sarah explained. "Middens can tell us a

great deal about a culture. Sometimes we find stuff like broken dishes or tools."

"What I'm hoping to find is a gouge," Patty said.

Zoë stared at her. "A gouge?"

Patty nodded. "Gouges were efficient woodworking tools, unique to the Maritime Archaic culture. We believe they were used in constructing wood framed houses."

"No one has ever found one?"

"There were a number of polished, unused gouges found in the cemetery. What I'm hoping to find is a broken or discarded one. If we find one it will be definite proof that we have found the habitation site."

"It's not gong to be easy," said Sarah. "It'll be like finding a needle in a haystack."

Patty laughed. "More like having a thousand haystacks and finding the right one with the right needle." She turned to look at Zoë. "The problem is that there are almost *too many* artifacts."

"Well," Abbey said. "Nice meeting you, Zoë. I should go back to work. I hope you'll consider working here. Maybe we can get together sometime?"

"Sure."

Soon everyone was back in the trenches, Sarah included. Zoë sat by a tree and watched.

Fog hovered over her head. Cold and miserable, she felt a wave of homesickness crash through her. She wanted to get away from these strange people. She wanted to go home. She wanted to visit an art gallery, go to the library. She wanted to hop on the subway and go to the Eaton Centre with Amber. Toronto felt as far away as Mars.

CHAPTER 4: The Tempest

"Full fathom five, thy father lies."
The Tempest

Zoë finished polishing the water taps in the bathroom and started on the full-length mirror. She could think of better ways to spend a Saturday morning. Not that she minded helping out, but polishing water taps seemed such a waste of time. Mum always said that no one would be remembered for their good housekeeping.

After she had scrubbed out the bathtub and basin, Zoë borrowed a pen and note pad from Mike's office and went upstairs to write a letter to Amber. When she walked in her room, she cast a critical eye over the paintings that lined the walls. Already she had painted more than half a dozen. The last time she had been this productive was just after Mum died. There were three paintings of the lighthouse that she had worked on at various times of the day. She had painted the ocean and even painted Laura while she was napping. *I'm getting better at showing depth and distance*, she told herself. Her art teacher had spent nearly three whole classes on this subject, and it was one of Zoë's favourites. The more she learned, the more excited she grew about art.

She sat on her bed to write.

June 30, 1997

Dear Amber:

I've been here over a week now, and it seems like a month. This place is even more isolated than I imagined. I feel as though I not only left Toronto, but Canada. Nothing here but a string of little villages, each one the same as the next. If I didn't have my painting, I'd die of boredom.

I am alone most of the day with Laura and Dora, her babysitter. We watch Oprah Winfrey and Dora's favourite soap opera, Guiding Light. *Dora keeps me entertained with stories. She told me about the time this famous French actress, Brigitte Bardow, came to Port au Choix with some other people to protest the seal hunt. The locals sent them to a place called Plum Point where they walked up to their knees in snow looking for plums.*

Sarah suffers from a serious case of what Mum would call perfectionitis. Nothing is allowed to be out of place in her house. Pots and pans are lined up neatly in the cupboards. Beds have to be made a certain way. Everything has to be dusted daily whether it needs it or not. She even irons her sheets and pillowcases!

Amber, there's something about Sarah and Mike that I just can't put my finger on. Remember how worried I was about them accepting me? The truth is, I don't know how they feel. Both Sarah and Mike seem ... I don't know ... detached. I could be a house pet for all I really seem to matter to them. I am sure Mike cares about me, though. Or, at least, I think he does.

I dread having to go to a new school. I met a girl my age. Her name is Abbey, and she works at an archaeological site. She wants me to work there as well. If I did, I could get extra credits at school. I can't imagine digging holes all day long, but I'm so bored I just might do it.

Take care, Amber, and give my love to the family.

Love, Zoë

After folding the letter and putting it in an envelope, Zoë got her jacket from the closet. She would walk to the post office. It would give her something to do. She had gone there with Sarah a couple of days ago, so she knew where it was. Most people in d'Arby Woods got their mail at the Port Saunders post office, but Sarah and Mike had theirs come to Port au Choix, no doubt because Sarah spent so much time there. It was quite a walk, but Zoë didn't mind.

It was chilly for the end of June, with a cold breeze blowing off the water. Zoë had only walked a short distance when a car stopped, and a man rolled down the window. "Need a ride, my love?" he called. He was old, maybe forty. He was wearing a jacket and baseball cap.

Zoë glared at him. Mum had warned her about getting into cars with strangers. She wanted to run, but she was so scared, she stood rooted to the spot, her heart pounding.

The man waited, and when Zoë didn't answer, he shrugged and drove off. *Pervert.* She should have written down his licence plate number and reported him to the police.

Zoë was about a kilometre from Port au Choix when a battered Dodge stopped. *Oh no*, she thought, *not another one.*

The driver was a woman with three little kids aboard. "Give you a lift?" she called.

"No thanks," Zoë said. As she watched the car drive off, it struck her that the first driver was probably just being friendly. She remembered Mike telling her that people around here really looked out for one another. She wished now she'd been more polite.

The main road curved along a rocky shore with houses on both sides. Zoë breathed in the pungency of salt water and fish. The houses were a mixture of one and two storey; some were plain wooden bungalows, while others were large brick structures with two-car garages. As she approached the post office, she realized she'd forgotten the mailbox key and would have to ask the postmistress if she could get their mail without it.

The postmistress was talking with a customer when Zoë arrived. "With yeh in a minute, my love," she called.

Zoë dropped her letter in the slot. As she waited, she looked out the tall windows. Seagulls wheeled over wharves that stretched over the water. Two small boys were rowing a wooden, flat-bottomed boat. A little girl was walking on the beach throwing rocks into the water. It looked like a scene from a Hallmark card. *Someday I'm going to come here and paint this*, she decided, taking in the scene.

"Will I see you tonight at Elaine's shower, Rita?" the customer asked.

"I'm gonna try to make it," the postmistress answered.

The customer left, and Rita turned her attention to Zoë.

"I left my mailbox key at home," she explained. "Is there any way I can get my mail?"

"No problem, my dear." And before Zoë had a chance to tell her the box number or even her name, Rita went into a side room and retrieved the mail.

"Thank you," Zoë said, accepting the pile of letters, cards, magazines, and stuffed manila envelopes. Near the bottom of the pile, she found a letter addressed to her from Amber. Just seeing the familiar handwriting brought a sharp pain of loneliness. Zoë waited until she was outside before opening it.

Dear Zoë:

Received your postcard. I hope things are getting better for you. Mom says it will take time for you to adjust. She sends her love. The police arrested Suzie Q. They took her to the hospital on Queen Street. After Aunt Reenie died, she never seemed the same. Mom went to see her at the hospital. She is very confused and keeps asking, "Who is going to take care of the baby now?"

I hope you will be able to come back for a visit soon, Zoë. We all miss you so much.

Love, Amber

Zoë shook her head, overcome with sadness. *Poor Suzie,* she thought. *What's going to become of her?*

No sooner had Zoë got home when the doorbell rang. She opened the door to a man with shoulder-length grey hair and a full beard. Zoë was so surprised she automatically stepped back.

"Zoë?" he said, stepping inside, and before she could say anything, he was hugging her. "I'm your Opa."

Mike came out of his study. "Dad? I didn't know you were back."

Opa held Zoë at arm's length. "Got in about an hour ago. Couldn't wait to meet her." He peered at her closely. "Who does she look like?"

"Sarah thinks she has the van der Post nose," Mike said. "What do *you* think?"

"Mmm!" Opa touched Zoë's nose with the tip of his index finger. "What I think is that I would like to take her out to lunch."

Zoë was so taken aback, she didn't know what to say.

"Tomorrow," he promised. "I'll pick you up at noon."

Amber would love this place! Zoë thought, looking around The Tempest. The waiters and waitresses were dressed like characters from Shakespeare's play with the same name. The restaurant was designed to look like an enchanted island with palm trees, buoys, pieces of driftwood, and a high blue ceiling with painted clouds. A fishnet ran along one wall decorated with multi-coloured Japanese fish floats. Outside a large bay window, long wharves jutted into the harbour. Rowboats, motorboats, and longliners dotted the water.

"I like it here," Zoë told Opa. "Sarah says you own this place."

"Not exactly. I helped get the restaurant started, and I have money invested."

A waiter dressed as a boatswain came by to take their orders. After carefully examining the menu, Zoë ordered lasagne.

"I'll have the stuffed salmon," Opa said, handing back the menu.

As Zoë watched the waiters and waitresses in their elaborate costumes, she was grateful for her grade nine Language Arts teacher, Mr. Bawdry. "The Bawd," as they called him, was a pompous Englishman who bragged about his degrees from Oxford. He believed Canadians were sadly lacking in culture and insisted his students read a number of Shakespeare's plays. Now, thanks to the Bawd, Zoë could identify most of the characters from *The*

Tempest. She knew the character in the yellow leotards was the prince, Ferdinand, and the stunted little fat man was the monster, Caliban. The pretty girl standing by the bar with silver sequins on her dress was Miranda, daughter of the magician, Prospero.

People kept stopping by their table to chat with Opa, and he proudly introduced Zoë as "my granddaughter from Toronto."

"Things have not been easy for you, Zoë," Opa said as they waited for their food. He shook his head. "Poor Maureen, gone so young."

Zoë lowered her head, struggling to hold back tears.

"No, the last seven months have been hard," she said. Her pain was never far from the surface. It took only a word or a memory to make it all come rushing back again.

Opa took his hand in hers and held it gently. "Things can only get better, with time."

Zoë doubted that, but she was grateful Opa understood the pain of her loss. Neither Mike nor Sarah had spoken a word about her mother.

The food came, and for a few minutes they ate in silence, listening to an elfin-faced girl play the piano and sing.

"That's Melanie," Opa explained. "One of my most promising students. She plays Ariel as if the part was written for her."

"She plays well."

"Yes." Opa peered at her. "So what have you been doing for excitement?"

"I spent yesterday at the beach, painting the ocean and the waves."

"Ah, a painter." He smiled at her. "Probably inherited your grandmother's talent."

Zoë fiddled with the straw in her glass of cola. She didn't like being compared to Ans.

Opa met her gaze. "Meet any new friends?"

"Not really. Well, there's Abbey, a girl who works at the archaeology site. Both she and Sarah want me to work there for the summer."

"And how do you feel about that?"

Zoë shrugged. "I don't know. It would give me a chance to meet other kids, I suppose."

Opa nodded. "I hear they are looking for the Maritime Archaic habitation site. It would be really exciting to be a part of that."

"Yes," Zoë said quietly. "I'm giving it some thought."

During lunch, Opa frequently peeked at his watch. Every time the door opened, he looked up from his plate. "Are you expecting someone?" Zoë asked.

"As a matter of fact, I am. Should have been here by now." He stroked his beard. "I can't tell you who it is because it's a surprise."

Before Zoë could say anything else, the boatswain came back to their table to clear away the dishes. "Would you like dessert?" he asked. "The specialty is blueberry pie."

"Then blueberry pie it shall be." Opa turned to Zoë. "The same?"

"Sounds good."

Moments later, the door opened and a woman stood in the doorway. She had short dark hair and was wearing a black turtleneck under a red blazer. Zoë saw her scanning the faces in the restaurant. Opa waved her over to their table. She smiled as she hurried toward them.

"Glad you could make it," Opa said. He stood up and pulled Zoë to her feet. She felt his arm encircle her waist. "Ans, I would like you to meet our granddaughter."

Zoë's mouth dropped open. This was Ans? She hadn't expected her to look so ordinary.

Ans gasped, and Zoë realized her grandmother was as stunned as she was. "Well, hello," Ans said, finding her voice. "Glad to finally meet you, Zoë." She reached a small, trembling hand toward her.

After a brief hesitation, Zoë took the proffered hand.

"Sit down," Opa said, pulling out a chair for her. "We just ordered dessert. Would you like something?"

"Some coffee perhaps, Alexander."

The boatswain returned with their pie.

"Could you bring some coffee?" Opa asked.

"Zoë," Ans began. "I was going to stop by to see you. I've been out of town."

Zoë nodded, feeling tongue-tied.

"Isn't she something?" Opa reached across the table and squeezed Zoë's hand. "An aspiring artist, no less."

Ans smiled at her.

Zoë took a forkful of pie, but found it too thick to go down her throat.

Ans sipped her coffee. "You must find this small outport quite different from Toronto."

"Yes." Zoë's hands were trembling, her stomach queasy. "Excuse me," she said. She rushed to the ladies' room, shaken and sick to her stomach. She barely made it into a stall before throwing up. Groaning, she slid to the floor and wrapped her arms around her knees.

She didn't know how long she stayed that way. After a while, she heard someone call her name. Reluctantly, she pulled herself to her feet and left the safety of the cubicle.

The girl with silver sequins was standing by the sink, arms folded across her chest. "Professor van der Post is worried about you," she said.

"Tell him I'll be out in a minute." Zoë felt like she was taking part in an audience participation play. The kind they used to put on at her elementary school in Toronto.

Miranda gave her an odd look. "Okay," she said.

Zoë couldn't stop trembling. She caught a glimpse of herself in the mirror and saw that her reflection was as pale as a porcelain platter.

When she went back to the restaurant, Opa was standing at the counter, paying the bill.

"You okay, love?" He squeezed her shoulder.

Mechanically, she nodded.

"Oma had to leave," he said. "She's going to try to drop by your house later this week."

Zoë glanced across the room at the palm trees and pieces of driftwood. The queasiness in her stomach had returned. She knew she would probably always feel uncomfortable around her grandmother. How could she not, considering how Ans treated her mother? Considering that Ans didn't want her to be born.

CHAPTER 5: Rough Seas

"I should sin to think but nobly of my grandmother."
The Tempest

"The Maritime Archaic Indians were the first people to come to Newfoundland," Farrah, the museum guide, was telling a group of tourists. "They arrived in Labrador nine thousand years ago. About five thousand years later, they crossed over to mainland Newfoundland."

Zoë, Mike, and Laura had stopped by the museum while they waited for Sarah to do business at the bank. Zoë had joined a guided tour. She was barely listening to the guide, however. Today, they were going to Cape Prosper to visit Ans. A week had passed since the incident at the restaurant. Although Zoë tried to come up with an excuse to stay behind, she knew she couldn't put it off forever. Mike's sister Anneke and her family were visiting from Nova Scotia, and they were all eager to meet her.

Farrah led them to a number of large glass showcases with skeletons inside. They looked as if they'd been buried sitting up, their bony legs pulled up to their chins. In the crook of their arms, they clutched stone spears, harpoons, and other tools and weapons. One of the skeletons, obviously a mother, tenderly embraced the fragmented skeleton of her child. Zoë felt such a rush of emotion, she blinked back tears.

"It's obvious this culture had a preoccupation with life after death," Farrah said. "They buried their dead with great ceremony. The red ochre found in the graves is a symbol of life. The tools and weapons found there suggest a belief in an afterlife similar to their life here on earth." She moved on to cases filled with weapons and tools. "The artifacts they left behind tell the story of their lives." She gestured to the display of woodworking tools. "Here we have slate knives, sturdy stone axes, gouges, and ivory adazes."

Zoë stared at the polished stone gouge. It was about six inches long with a concave edge. So that was what Patty and her team were fixed on finding. She could see how it would be used as a tool for making building materials.

"Judging by their barbed harpoons, bayonets, spears, and lances, we know they must have been skilled hunters," Farrah continued. "Awls, bone needles, and scrapers made from caribou bones were also found in the graves—tools used to prepare and make clothing from animal hides."

The guide talked at length about how animal hides were made into clothing before moving on to another showcase filled with combs and pins, decorated with heads of birds and other animals. "Art was very much a part of their lives …"

Despite this mention of art, Zoë found her mind drifting. She felt a wave of resentment recalling the conversation she'd had with Mike this morning. She had balked when he told her about the trip to Cape Prosper, had asked if she could stay home. "Zoë, there's no reason in the world you should feel uncomfortable around your Oma," he had said. *She didn't want me to be born,* Zoë wanted to say, but she remained silent.

No doubt Ans had told him she'd sensed Zoë's uneasiness. *Well too bad,* she thought. *I can't help it if this woman makes me uncomfortable.*

By the time Zoë got back to the visitor's centre, Sarah had returned from the bank, rain dripping from her hair. "Enjoy your tour, Zoë?"

"Yes, it was interesting."

"It's like looking through a window back in time," Sarah said excitedly. She pulled up the hood of Laura's raincoat. "Well, I suppose we should be going."

Rain was coming down hard by the time they boarded the van. "Must be a wild day on the cape," Mike said, as he backed the car out of the museum parking lot.

"Every day is wild on Cape Prosper," said Sarah.

They drove past tiny outports with fishing boats tied up at the wharves. The only sound was the swishing of the windshield wipers. Laura sang "Itsy, Bitsy Spider," and Zoë joined in.

"Some spiders will never learn," Mike muttered after they had sung the song for about the fifteenth time. Only Zoë heard; Laura had her eyes closed, head nodding forward.

Zoë felt her stomach tighten as they pulled into the driveway of Ans's small bungalow beside the sea. Opa had named the place Cape Prosper. Zoë could hear the roar of the ocean from inside the car. There were flowers planted in the yard and large wooden shoes filled with tulips on the front lawn. Mike once said his mother had a green thumb and loved bringing things to life.

"Anneke and Mark are here." Mike gestured to the blue station wagon parked alongside Ans's little red Topaz. The curtains parted and two small faces appeared in the window.

Ans met them at the door. "Hello, darling," she said to Zoë. "I'm so glad you came."

Zoë stepped back, afraid she might try to hug her.

"Hello, Ans," she said politely.

Laura was awake now, stretching out her arms. "Oma," she cooed happily.

A tall woman with cropped blonde hair came to greet them.

"Zoë," Mike said, "this is your Aunt Anneke."

She grasped Zoë's hand warmly. "I've been looking forward to meeting you," she said. "Come meet your Uncle Mark and your cousins." She led her into the kitchen where a short dark-haired man sat at the table with two children. A board game had been set out.

Uncle Mark rose to take her hand. "I've heard a lot about you, Zoë" he said.

Anneke turned to the children, a girl about seven and a boy who looked to be about a year younger. They stared at Zoë with wide eyes. "And these are your cousins, Erin and Andrew."

They wore identical overalls, and Erin's hair was so short that at first Zoë mistook her for a boy. It gave her an odd feeling meeting relatives she never knew existed.

"Are you Uncle Mike's cousin too?" the boy asked.

"That's dumb, Andrew," Erin said scornfully.

Anneke ran her fingers through her short blonde hair. "Now kids, no bickering." She winked at Zoë. "You don't want to make a bad impression on your new cousin."

Ans came into the kitchen, followed by Sarah. Soon everyone was talking at once.

Zoë followed Mike into a large living room where flowers bloomed in pots on tables and windowsills. There were little wooden shoes and windmills on the mantle. Black and white and colour photos adorned the walls, some old and cracked with age.

"Know who this is?" Mike pointed out a black and white photograph of a young woman standing in a field. She was wearing a lace cap and was obviously pregnant.

Zoë shrugged.

"That's your Oma. Taken shortly before I was born."

"And here's your great-grandfather." Mike pointed to a faded photograph of a man standing in a pasture surrounded by cows. In the background was a windmill against a white expanse of sky.

Zoë stared at the photograph. More relatives. Beside her great-grandfather's picture was a painting of a young woman. She was struck by the woman's dark eyes and high cheekbones. She was about to ask Mike about her when Sarah called to him from the kitchen.

The top of the piano and the mantle were cluttered with recent photos—pictures of Erin, Andrew, and Laura. Zoë was surprised to see her own picture among the others, one she had sent Mike and Sarah from Toronto.

She wandered into another room off the living room. Ans's studio, she realized. The room had a large bay window that looked out on the ocean; Zoë could see great waves crashing against the shore. A half-finished oil painting stood on an easel. Paintbrushes and tubes were scattered on a nearby table along with tins of turpentine, linseed oil, and a wooden spatula smeared with paint.

Zoë examined the painting, trying to imagine what it might become. A landscape perhaps? Or maybe even a person. At this stage, it could be anything. She would have to see more before she could even guess what it might be.

Another of Ans's paintings stood near the window. She had painted the ocean as it appeared on a calm day. *A Promise of Calm Seas* was written on a sticky note, stuck to the easel. Was it the title? Zoë wondered. The sea in the painting was tranquil, and there were fishing boats and sailboats in the bay. In the background was a small island with a miniature red and white lighthouse. She looked through the window, but it was too stormy to see the island, and she wondered if it even existed. *Ans is a very good painter*, Zoë had to admit.

Reproductions of paintings were hung on the studio walls, many of them by artists who used a method called *trompe l'oeil*. Zoë had studied this technique in her art appreciation course. She found it fascinating how artists gave the illusion of depth or motion to their paintings.

"It's a trick of the eye that gives the illusion of reality," Zoë's instructor had said. Judging from the paintings in Ans's studio, it was obvious she was partial to this method as well. Was it just coincidence that she and Ans shared similar interests in art?

From the kitchen came the muted sounds of voices and laughter, the clatter of dishes. Something smelled delicious—lasagne, or was it spaghetti sauce? Given the choice, Zoë would rather be alone, but it would be rude to keep to herself. Reluctantly, she went to join the others.

The table, covered with a white linen tablecloth, was laden with homemade jams, cheese, and scones. There was chili and lasagne, bowls of fruit and dips. Zoë took a chair across the table from Mike and Sarah.

Ans came to the table carrying a basket of rolls, fresh from the oven. "Erin, darling, I've baked an extra batch of cheese rolls just for you."

Anneke shook her head. "Mom, you're spoiling her."

Ans placed the basket in front of Erin. "The first grandchild is bound to be a little spoiled."

An awkward silence settled around the table. Mike shot Zoë a sympathetic look. Ans's face turned red. "Of course, I have four grandchildren now," she gushed. "Four lovely grandchildren."

Zoë pretended not to notice. She wanted only to go home.

CHAPTER 6: Searching for the Habitation Site

"The sea mocks our frustrate search on land."
The Tempest

Zoë breathed in the earthy, mossy smell of black peat as she scraped her trowel along the walls of the trench she shared with Abbey. It had been almost a week since she came to work at the site, and it really wasn't that bad. At times it got boring, going for hours without finding anything. But she enjoyed the companionship she shared with her team members.

Her trowel hit something hard, and with great care, she removed the earth surrounding it. She felt a tinge of disappointment after discovering it was only a rock. "Not finding much today," she said, speaking her thoughts aloud.

"It's much better in Phillip's Garden," Abbey said. "Out there you find all kinds of interesting stuff."

"Maybe we should have searched near there for the habitation site?"

Abbey shook her head. "Patty has ruled out that site. The Maritime Archaic Indians preferred sheltered inlets. Most likely they would have chosen a site that had a view of open water in a number of directions. And the site would probably have a view of the cemetery."

Zoë listened with interest, realizing the chosen location wasn't random.

"They would also have needed fresh water for drinking," Abbey continued, "so the habitation site would be near ponds or lakes."

"But how do we know this is the right place?"

"We don't. Patty says it's just an educated guess. The site could just as well be at the other end of Port au Choix. It could be underwater. The sea has risen in the four thousand years since the Maritime Archaic Indians lived here."

We could end up not finding anything, Zoë thought. Sarah had told her about all the years Patty and her team had spent looking for the habitation site. Discouraged, she put down her trowel. Could all this digging be for nothing? Now that she had started working here, she really wanted to be part of solving the great Maritime Archaic mystery. To her surprise, Zoë had started taking an interest in the prehistoric cultures at Port au Choix. She found herself asking questions and had even picked up a couple of books at the museum. The fact that other people had lived here thousands of years ago held a kind of fascination for her.

"Oh my God! Oh my God!" Zoë was jolted out of her thoughts by the shrieks coming from a trench across from her.

"Looks like Jessie found something," Abbey said. She climbed out of the trench, and Zoë followed. Jessie Chambers was a grade eleven student who had come to work at the site just a couple of days ago.

"Oh my God!"

By the time the girls reached Jessie's pit, Patty was already there, along with a number of other team members who had gathered around.

"For heaven's sake, Jessie. It's a rock," Patty said.

"How was I s'posed to know?" Jessie pouted. With her freckled face and her hair in pigtails, she looked about twelve.

"Can't imagine what would happen if she found something of real value," Abbey whispered.

Patty looked at her watch. "Lunch time," she announced.

Slowly, the team members walked away, some to their vehicles, others to pick up boxed lunches they had left in various places throughout the site. Zoë could tell they were disappointed by Jessie's false alarm.

Zoë picked up her backpack from under a tree. Except for The Tempest, which was miles away, there were no restaurants in the area. Sometimes she and Abbey walked to the grocery store to buy prepared sandwiches, but most of the time she ate the lunches Dora packed for her.

Abbey spread a blanket on the ground, and Zoë went to join her. By now the team was sitting in a circle on the grass. They pulled sandwiches and drinks from boxes and paper bags. Jessie had removed her hat and was leaning against the fence.

Zoë opened the square cookie tin Dora used to pack her lunch. She found an egg salad sandwich, a small carton of juice, an apple, and a chocolate bar.

At that moment, Jake Loyal came out of his house carrying a plate covered with tin foil. Zoë looked at her watch and saw it was eight minutes past twelve. Jake arrived the same time every day, usually with cookies or some other treat for the workers. He was about sixty years old with grey, thinning hair. He wore baggy pants with suspenders and a red plaid shirt. "Any luck?" he asked as he approached.

"Found nothing important, Jake," Patty said. She eyed the plate he was carrying. "What did you bring us today?"

"Peanut butter balls," he said, removing the tin foil. "Made them this morning." He laid the dish on a large flat rock. "Help yourself, everyone."

"Jake, you're spoiling us," Patty exclaimed. She opened a plastic container. "Would you like to share a sandwich with me?"

"No thanks, Patty. Got company coming." He looked at his watch. "Any minute now."

Jake started up the path toward his house. He had only gone a little way when he turned, spreading his arms wide "Just imagine," he said, "thousands of years ago the Maritime Archaic Indians had full run of this place. What a time they musta had, wha?"

Jessie stomped out her cigarette. She walked over to the rock, picked up a peanut butter ball, and put it in her mouth. "Too bad you weren't around then Jake," she said. "You could have made them treats. Mmm, delicious. Thanks, Jake."

"Thanks Jake," the others echoed.

Jake nodded. "If you needs anything," he said, "anything a'tall, let me know. My door is always open."

"He's so sweet," Abbey whispered, as they watched him walk away. "Patty was afraid he'd be upset with so many of us digging up his land. But he's welcomed us with open arms."

"I think he enjoys our company," Zoë said.

Abbey nodded. "He's probably lonely. His wife died less than a year ago, and he misses her. Must be really hard for him."

"Yes," Zoë agreed. "It's hard to lose someone you love." She turned her head quickly so Abbey wouldn't see her tears.

CHAPTER 7: Untold Truths

"Your tale, sir, would cure deafness."
The Tempest

"Zoë wants to get off at her grandfather's house," Abbey told her mother. They had just come from Kepple Island, and Mrs. Reid had picked them up at the wharf at Port Saunders.

"No problem," she said. "I'll drop you off on the way."

"Thanks," Zoë said. She leaned back in the seat of the small car. She had been in Newfoundland for nearly six weeks now. She had settled into her work at the archaeological site and liked the routine. She liked getting up in the morning, having someplace to go. She enjoyed her co-workers. By now, some of the team members were starting to get discouraged, but Zoë just wanted to dig.

Zoë still missed Toronto, but things had improved as she settled into her new life. She and Abbey had become fast friends, and Abbey's friends accepted her. In the evenings they enjoyed bonfires on the beach, roasting wieners and marshmallows. Other times, like today, they rowed out to Kepple Island. Zoë sometimes wondered what they thought of her—this strange girl from "away" who had never been in a fishing boat.

"Here we are," said Mrs. Reid as she pulled into Opa's driveway.

"Don't forget Nick's party on Saturday," Abbey said.

Party? Zoë had not been invited and was about to say so when she remembered that there were no invitations, no RSVPs. If someone was having a party, you just showed up. "Thanks for reminding me, Abbey. I'll try to make it."

Zoë hurried up the driveway. She hadn't seen her grandfather in over a week. He'd be leaving for Corner Brook soon and would only be around on weekends.

Opa opened the door, a phone to his ear, long cord trailing behind him. Waving Zoë inside, he gave her a quick hug. "Five," he mouthed, holding up five fingers. "With theatre it's different," he said into the phone. "An audience accepts what they see. Disbelief is suspended."

He plugged in the kettle and, without a break in the conversation, got mugs and tea bags from the shelf.

Sensing the conversation might take some time, Zoë wandered into the living room. Shelves overflowed with books; they were stacked on tables and piled high on the floor. The walls were covered with framed paintings and photographs. There was a small painted portrait of a young woman not much older than Zoë. She looked closely at the painting, realizing it was the same woman she'd seen in a painting at Ans's house. In this portrait, she was painted from a different angle, but there was no doubt it was the same person. Who was she? A relative? She must remember to ask Opa.

A new photograph was hanging above the fireplace, and she realized it was the Diane Arbus print Opa had shipped from an art gallery in New York City. Zoë stepped back to get a better look. *Nothing special about this one*, she thought, taking in the lake with trees in the foreground. The title, *A Lobby in a Building, New York City 1966* was displayed on a small brass tag attached to the painting. Peering closer, Zoë noticed a dark wooden panel and a wall plug at the bottom corner of the photograph. It was not a photograph of a landscape as Zoë first thought, but a photograph of a photograph of a landscape. It was actually the wallpaper in the lobby of what looked like a hotel. She knew the print had cost Opa hundreds of dollars. Why would he spend so much money on something like that?

"Well, you take care now," she heard Opa say from the kitchen. Realizing the conversation was about to end, Zoë went to join him there.

In the hallway, she nearly collided with Ans who came out of the bathroom wearing a white bathrobe, her hair wet and uncombed. It was obvious she had just stepped out of the shower. "Oh, hello, Zoë," she said. "I didn't hear you come in."

In the kitchen, Opa was hanging up the phone. He turned to Zoë. "Sorry to abandon you, love. One of my drama students." He looked at Ans. "Your Oma was in town doing some shopping and decided to drop by."

Ans put a hand on Zoë's shoulder. "I'm glad you came," she said. "Matter of fact, I was going to go visit you tonight. Our visits have been so brief."

Before Zoë had a chance to respond, Opa rubbed his hands together. "Well, tea's on," he announced.

"I'll be back in a moment," Ans said, and disappeared upstairs.

"I can't stay long," Zoë said, struggling to come up with an excuse to leave.

"Have a seat," Opa said. "Your Oma brought carrot cake. I'm dying to sink my teeth into it." He didn't seem to notice Zoë's disquiet.

Zoë took a seat at the table. Opa poured tea and cut up the cake. He took down plates from the cupboard.

Ans returned moments later wearing a blue sweatsuit, her hair neatly combed. She took a seat across from Zoë. "You'll soon have a birthday, Zoë."

No thanks to you. "September fifteenth."

"How do you think you'll like spending your birthday at the cottage?" Opa put three spoons on the table.

"What cottage?"

"Our cottage at Beothuk Lake. Didn't they tell you?"

Ans smiled. "Alexander, I think you've just given away a carefully planned surprise."

Opa's hand flew to his beard. "Oh, dear. I've done it again. No wonder they kicked me out of the army."

"We're going to the cottage?" A couple of weeks ago, Zoë had spent a night at Beothuk Lake with Sarah and Mike after they learned a window had been broken and went to check it out. She fell in love with the cottage, a simple A-frame with a large deck overlooking the lake.

"Thanks," she said, her eyes on Opa.

Ans took a package of cigarettes from her purse. "You really ought to thank Mike and Sarah. Especially Sarah." She laughed. "Sarah is about as comfortable in the woods as a bear on a city street." She fumbled for her matches. "You don't mind if I smoke, do you, dear?"

"It hurts my throat," Zoë said, and felt a stab of satisfaction as she watched Ans put the cigarette back in the package.

Opa took a seat at the table. "Don't let on I told you about the secret plan for your birthday," Opa said. "Act like it's a big surprise. Jump up and down if you have to."

Zoë smiled.

"How's the digging?" Opa asked.

"We still haven't found the habitation site. Patty is very disappointed."

Opa licked icing from his fingers. "There's still time."

"Yes," Zoë agreed, "but Patty is starting to become desperate. Soon we will have to stop digging for the season."

"You must come visit me at Cape Prosper, Zoë," Ans said, changing the topic. "I'll take you out in my boat."

Zoë didn't answer.

"The seas have been rough for a long time now." Ans stared off into the distance, as if she was talking to herself. "But the ocean always gets calmer."

"Did you enjoy your day?" Mike asked as Zoë climbed in the van.

"Kepple Island is great," Zoë said, buckling her seat belt. "Maurice and Wayne brought guitars and we sang. Abbey and I walked around the island and saw a pod of whales. Next time I go out there, I'm going to bring my art supplies. I've painted the island from our dining room window, but it would be neat to paint it up close."

She glanced at Mike and saw he was smiling. "Zoë, your art is more than a hobby, isn't it?"

"Yes," she said, pleased that Mike understood.

"The scenery is fantastic from the island."

Zoë nodded. "Next time though, I'll take a sweater. It can get chilly out there."

Mike backed the van out of the driveway. "I bet. It's always chilly on the water, and we haven't had much of a summer." He peered at Zoë. "Must be quite a change from Toronto."

"Yes," she agreed, "but I don't mind. I don't like the heat."

"Your mother was the same way." Mike smiled at the memory. "She was always uncomfortable in July and August and couldn't wait for fall."

Ever since she arrived in Newfoundland, Zoë had wanted to ask Mike about his relationship with her mother, and now the opportunity had presented itself. "What happened between you and Mum?" she summoned up the courage to ask.

"Happened?" Mike echoed.

"Why did you break up?"

Mike stopped to let some children cross the street. "We were going to get married," he said, "even though my parents were against it."

"Ans wanted Mum to have an abortion," Zoë said.

Mike looked at her. "Is that what Reenie told you?"

"She said that's why she left."

Mike shook his head. "No, that's not true. Your grandmother was upset about the pregnancy, and she made it known. I'm not sure what she wanted Reenie to do. I don't even think she thought it through herself. But your mother was very hurt, and rightfully so. I think she might have believed my mother wanted her to have an abortion. We had a big fight, and she left." He came to a yield sign and slowed down. "I wish now I had gone after her. But I was young and full of arrogance. I didn't know where she had gone. I waited for her to call me, but she never did. Months later a friend of hers called, saying Reenie had had a miscarriage, that she wanted nothing more to do with me."

Zoë's eyes went wide with surprise.

"When your Aunt Caroline tracked down my parents to tell them about Reenie's death, she was stunned to learn I was still alive." He turned to look at her. "And of course, I was just as shocked to find out Reenie had not had a miscarriage as I'd been led to believe." Mike frowned. "I must have really hurt your mother for her to go to such extremes, to tell such lies. It's hard to even imagine her doing such things. She was not a person who was deceptive or malicious."

They rode in silence for a few moments. "I had no idea, Zoë," Mike said, shaking his head. "No idea at all that you even existed."

Zoë was quiet, thinking over everything Mike had just revealed. Could it be that Mum was wrong about Ans? Could she have misunderstood her? Family is important, Mum always said. *If she truly believed that,* Zoe wondered, *why would she deprive me of a father and grandparents?*

CHAPTER 8: School

> "Hast thou not dropped from heaven?"
> *The Tempest*

It was not yet 6:30 AM, but Zoë decided to get up anyway. During the night she'd been restless and had awakened twice. In less than three hours, she would be starting high school. She looked at the clothes she had set out on a chair the night before. The jeans were stiff and new, the sweater had a price tag dangling from the sleeve. Sarah had taken her to Corner Brook a few days ago to buy new clothes and school supplies. While Zoë was at the mall trying on clothes, Sarah took Laura to get ice cream, leaving her credit card with the sales clerk. "Pick out whatever you need and charge it," she told Zoë. For forty-five minutes, she had tried on clothes. She left the store with two pairs of jeans, two tops, a sweater, and a suede jacket. It was a strange experience for her; Mum bought all their clothes at thrift shops. Afterwards, they went to Staples and bought the rest of her school supplies, including a new backpack. Sarah had suggested she pick up canvases, brushes, and other art supplies, too. *Sarah is good to me*, Zoë had to admit. But she would like to be closer to her stepmother. Closer to Mike as well. But they kept their distance. *Maybe that will come in time*, she told herself.

God, I look terrible, Zoë thought, studying her reflection in the bathroom mirror. Her cheeks were pale, and dark shadows smudged her eyes from lack of sleep. She dressed quickly and went downstairs. A cup of tea would help settle her queasy stomach, she decided.

She carried the tea back to her room, even though she knew Sarah didn't allow food or drink in the bedroom. She put the cup down on her night table and began stuffing her backpack with binders, loose leaf, pens, pencils, notebooks, and her new calculator.

From her closet, Zoë got out a box that had arrived yesterday from Aunt Caroline. She'd been out all day with Abbey and their friends, so she hardly had a chance to go through it. There were report cards, a random assortment of photographs, old Christmas and Valentine cards. She found pictures she had drawn as a child, a poem she'd written for her mother's birthday. Among the photographs was a Polaroid picture of her mother with two other women. Zoë picked it up and examined it, a pang of sadness washing over her. It was still hard to accept that she would never see her mother again. She turned the photograph over. "Rusty, JoJo, and Reenie" was written on the back.

There were three journals among the items. Zoë flipped through the yellowing pages that carried the dank, musty smell of Aunt Caroline's basement. One of the entries was dated 1986. Zoë would have been four years old at the time. "I do not know what I would do without Zoë," her mother had written. "She makes my life worth living." Tears stung her eyes. In another entry her mother wrote: "It breaks my heart that she will never know her father." *Why?* Zoë wondered. *Mike would have provided for me. How could Mum have kept me from him all those years?*

She continued reading, hardly aware of people laughing and talking outside. Kids were drifting out of their homes on their way to catch the school bus. A car door opened and closed. Downstairs, she heard the doorbell. Zoë glanced at the digital clock next to her bed and saw that it was 8:15 AM. She put the journals back in the box, picked up her backpack, and hurried downstairs.

She was more than a little surprised to see Josh sitting at the kitchen table, a mug of tea in front of him. He met Zoë's gaze, his dark eyes as luminous as tinted glass. He was even more handsome in person. He was wearing a blue sweater with a shirt of a lighter blue underneath. What was he doing here so early in the morning? He'd been fishing with his father for most of the summer, and she hadn't seen much of him. There were the odd times when she'd seen him through the window when he was working on his car, walking the neighbour's dog, or playing with his brothers.

"I've asked Josh to drive you to school," Mike said. "I'd drive you myself, except I'm needed at the hospital."

"But I told Abbey I'd meet her at the bus stop."

"The bus already left." Mike put a glass of juice in front of her. "Ten minutes ago. Sorry. Sarah and I overslept, even Laura. That sometimes happens on Dora's day off."

"I must have misunderstood," Zoë said. "I thought the bus left at 8:45."

"It's OK. Besides, Josh can show you around," Mike said as he hustled around the kitchen, preparing a quick breakfast. "Introduce you to some of his friends."

Zoë nodded, although she'd already met most of the kids their age through Abbey.

Josh gave her a quick smile, showing teeth that were white and even.

Zoë pulled out a kitchen chair and sat down across from him, embarrassed that Mike had called him. Although the school bus stopped at d'Arby Woods, the school was in walking distance, and she could have made her own way. Still, it was a good five kilometres away; she probably would have been late.

Mike's beeper went off, and he headed toward the telephone leaving Zoë alone with Josh.

"Mike tells me you're in grade ten," he said.

Zoë nodded. "That's right."

"I'm going into grade eleven."

"I was hoping the school would have an art program."

Josh shook his head. "Art's not on the curriculum, but your grandfather has been trying to involve the students with drama." He drained his cup and took it to the sink. "Ready?"

Zoë got her jacket from the closet and picked up her backpack. She'd normally have some toast for breakfast, but today she was too nervous to eat. She had only managed a couple of swallows of her juice.

"Have a good day at school," Mike said, coming back into the kitchen.

"Would you like for me to drive her home?" Josh asked.

"I can walk or take the bus," Zoë said. Having Josh pick her up because she missed the bus was one thing, but she certainly didn't want him to think Mike was babying her.

Mike helped her into her jacket; Josh fished in his pocket for his car keys.

His car was parked in the driveway, a white Dodge Shadow

with a lot of rust spots. He opened the driver's door, reached across the seat and opened the passenger door. "It only opens from this side," he explained.

Zoë got in and closed the door. Josh turned the key in the ignition and fiddled with the dial until he found some good music. "Mike tells me you work at the archaeological site. How's that working out?"

"I'm enjoying it, actually." She smiled. "There's always that chance of finding something exciting."

Josh nodded. "My mom is interested in archaeology. I enjoy hearing her talk about ancient cultures and civilization. I never thought it could be that interesting."

In the school parking lot, a red car pulled up beside them. "Hey Josh, what's up?" A guy shouted through the open window. He parked the car, got out, and came toward them.

"Zack?" Josh turned off the engine. "Haven't seen you all summer."

"Been away. How 'bout you?"

"Busy. Helping dad with the fish." Josh got out of the car and opened the door for Zoë. "This is Zoë," he said to Zack. "She's from away."

"Hi," Zack said. He had carrot-red hair and a wide grin. "What grade are you going in?"

"Tenth."

"Grade ten? So am I."

"Zack loves grade ten," Josh said dryly. "Loves it so much, he came back a second time."

Zack punched him on the shoulder. Turning to Zoë, he said. "If you like, I can show you where the grade ten classroom is."

Grade ten classroom? What was he talking about? This wasn't elementary school. Even in junior high, students changed classes.

"Thanks." She followed Zack up a flight of stairs.

"Let me know how your classes go," Josh called.

Zoë nodded, gazing at his handsome, smiling face. He was being polite, she realized.

Showing kindness to the neighbour's girl. Mike had asked him to drive her to school, after all.

Abbey was standing near the door, talking to Ashley Lawless and another girl Zoë hadn't met. She waved as Zoë approached.

Zack wandered over to one of the lockers to talk to a friend.

"Good morning, Zoë," Abbey said. "I thought we were going to meet at the bus stop."

"Sorry. I was confused about the time."

"Oh well. Next time. This is Zoë," Abbey told her friends. "Zoë, I don't think you've met Isabella. She was away all summer visiting her aunt in St. John's."

"Hi," Zoë said, and Isabella nodded and smiled. She was a tall girl with stringy blonde hair and braces.

"Zoë lives in the subdivision," Abbey said. "She's Dr. Porter's stepdaughter. She works at the site with me."

"So you live in that house across the street from Josh Carter?" Isabella asked.

Zoë nodded. "Across the street and two doors down."

"Isabella's got it real bad for Josh," Ashley said.

"Well … he is kinda cute," Isabella said.

The bell rang and Zoë followed them to the grade ten classroom. Instead of the students going from class to class, the teachers came to them. There were no drama or art classes, but the school did have a music program. There were only two computers, which took forever to log onto. The first class was math with Miss House, who looked to be no older than her students.

The second class was social studies with Mr. Bean, a tall thin man with a lisp. After giving an overview of what they'd be covering this term, he said, "Most of the term's work will be based on an assignment," he said. "Worth sixty per cent of your mark." He looked around the classroom. "I want each of you to choose a partner."

There was a murmur of voices and a shuffling of desks. Zoë felt a pang of misgiving, remembering how she and Amber always did their projects together. A soft tap on her shoulder jolted her back to the present. Abbey stood beside her. "Would you like to be my partner?" she asked.

"Thanks," Zoë said gratefully.

"I want you to do an extensive study on a North American aboriginal hunting and gathering group," Mr. Bean said after they had paired off. He rubbed his fingers through his thinning dark hair. "Our coast has a rich anthropological history," he continued, and although he spoke to no one in particular, his gaze was on Zoë. "The Paleoeskimo, Groswater Paleoeskimo, Beothuk, and Maritime Archaic Indians have all roamed our shores. Further down the coast at L'Anse aux Meadows, an ancient Viking site was discovered. After you have decided which group you want to work on, come see me." He looked around the classroom. "Questions?"

Mr. Bean spent most of the period talking about the assignment. He had launched into a discussion about the Paleoeskimo when the bell rang for lunch.

"We could do something on the Maritime Archaic Indians," Abbey said as they walked outside. "Maybe on how art played a role in their lives."

"Great idea!" Zoë said. She remembered from her tour at the museum that a lot of art objects were found in the graves.

"Mr. Bean's an awesome teacher," Abbey said. "My brother had him last year. There will be at least one visit to the museum."

Abbey talked non-stop, her prattle putting Zoë at ease. Although she knew a lot of the kids by now, she was still a little nervous about starting high school. But by the end of lunch and the start of afternoon classes, her nervousness had vanished.

When Zoë left the classroom that afternoon, she spotted Josh in the hallway, standing near the stairs. She started toward him, eager to tell him about her day. But before she got to him, two other girls approached him. One of them, a pretty blonde, whispered something in his ear. Zoë watched as he playfully made a grab for her scarf.

Surprised by the jolt of jealousy she felt, Zoë turned and hurried in the other direction.

CHAPTER 9: Illusions

"Let us not burden our remembering with
a heaviness that's gone."
The Tempest

The cool crisp smells of early September drifted into the open cottage window. Zoë watched as a squirrel scrambled across a large branch. From far off came the trilling of birds. Through the bare trees, she could see the lake as smooth as cellophane. It was hard to feel sad on a day like this. The pain she had felt for so long was nothing more than a dull ache now. She knew she would always miss Mum, but days like this made her loss easier to bear.

Zoë turned away from the window and went back to the letter she was writing to Amber. Chewing on her pen, she read what she had written. It was long and rambling. *The big news,* she added, *is that I am going to have a little brother or sister. Sarah is pregnant. The baby isn't due until March, but she already has the nursery ready. I used to envy you, Amber, because you had so many brothers and sisters and I was an only child. Now I have a sister and another brother or sister on the way.*

I never thought I would say this, but I like it here. The people are very friendly. They invite me into their homes as if I was family. The school is very small, and I know all the kids already. I also enjoy working at the site. It can be boring at times, but whenever we find something it's all worth it.

Please write soon.

Love, Zoë

From downstairs came the rattle of pots and dishes. Sarah was preparing chicken in tomato sauce—Zoë's favourite meal. She had offered to help, but Sarah had insisted that she be free on her birthday. "How many times do you get to turn fifteen?" she asked. "Go for a walk, read a book. I'll take care of things here."

Outside, she could hear Laura shrieking with laughter. Zoë turned back to the window and saw that Mike had buried her under a pile of leaves. She smiled now watching them. Little wonder Laura didn't look like Mike or Sarah: Her sister was adopted. She found that out the same day she learned Sarah's big news. Mike had taken Zoë and Laura shopping, and when they returned, Sarah was sitting in the rocker, staring into space. Mike asked if she was okay, and she burst into tears. "I'm pregnant," she said. Later, Mike explained that the doctors believed Sarah could never have a baby of her own.

When Zoë went downstairs, Sarah was standing by the counter pouring rice into a measuring cup. A maternity dress billowed around her flat stomach like a deflated balloon.

"Oh there you are," Sarah said, as if Zoë had been misplaced.

"Can I help?" she offered again.

"There's not much to do, really." Sarah took pieces of chicken from the fridge and rubbed garlic over the skin. "Mike is keeping Laura out of my hair. I'd rather you spent your birthday having fun."

"Well, in that case, maybe I'll row across the lake."

"The life jackets are in the closet in the foyer." Sarah turned on the oven and checked to see if the light had come on.

Zoë pulled a sweatshirt over her turtleneck. The sun was warm, but she knew it got cool and breezy on the water. "I want to thank you and Mike for this weekend," she said suddenly. "I am really enjoying my time here." Somehow, she felt it was necessary to let Sarah know she appreciated her efforts.

Sarah smiled. "You really like it here?"

"Oh, yes." Zoë looked around the large room, at the brick fireplace that ran along one wall. The floors were dark hardwood with rugs scattered about. The furniture was old and faded, the chairs around the table mismatched. There were shelves filled with books, and Diane Arbus prints adorned the walls. *Interesting but creepy,* Zoë thought as she studied *A Woman with her Baby Monkey, N.J. 1971.* In the photograph, a woman was holding a monkey dressed in baby clothes.

"I hope you like blue cheese dressing." Sarah washed her hands and brought out radishes, lettuce, and carrots from the fridge.

"Blue cheese is fine." Zoë put a few things in her backpack and went to get a life jacket from the closet.

Walking down the well-worn path to the boat, she felt light and carefree. Leaves the colour of dried mustard crunched under her feet. The sun was bright, and all around her were the smells and sounds of autumn. Just as she was about to untie the boat, Laura came running up to her, red rubber boots flopping on her small feet. Mike was close behind, also wearing tall boots. Laura stopped to throw a handful of rocks into the lake. She had on a blue hooded jacket, red curls held in place with little barrettes shaped like crayons.

"Goin' crusin'?" Mike said as he got closer.

Laura held up a rock. "Wock," she announced.

"Laura, I didn't even hear you get up this morning."

"We sure did." Mike laughed. "Six o'clock sharp."

Zoë stepped into the boat, and after she was seated, Mike gave it a push. There was the sound of pebbles crunching along the bottom, and then she was drifting out into the lake. "Drive carefully," Mike called after her.

She grabbed the oars and started to row.

Mike and Laura waved to her from shore. When Mike reached for Laura's small hand, Zoë was painfully reminded that her father wasn't around when she was that age. As she watched them walk down the beach, a pang of longing opened up inside her. She looked across the lake at the stunted dying trees, resentment welling inside her. A sudden breeze came up, ruffling the surface of the water. The raucous cawing of a crow could be heard in the distance.

As she watched Mike and Laura's receding figures, Zoë thought of the rundown rooming houses she had lived in with her mother. Rooms where they had to cook their meals on hot plates. Dumps where she had to share the bathroom with strangers. Waking up in the middle of the night to find some stranger's pee in the toilet. Going hungry because she didn't have lunch money. Since coming to live with Mike and Sarah, she never had to worry about food or clothing. Sarah complained all the time because she couldn't get things here that she could in the city, but she cooked great meals.

As Laura and Mike disappeared from sight, Zoë took a deep steadying breath. She stopped rowing, resting the oars across her knees in an attempt to sort out her tumble of emotions. Ahead of her, the water looked calm and unruffled. Further down the lake was a little cove. Picking up her oars, she rowed toward it.

After pulling the boat up on the beach, Zoë found a place under a shady tree where she could sit quietly and read. It was so peaceful, only the occasional trilling of a bird broke the silence. Opening her backpack, she took out her mother's journals. They were in random order, and she chose one with a picture of a sunflower on the cover. The handwriting was small and wobbly, obviously written during the early stages of Mum's pregnancy, before she took her calligraphy course.

A lady came by today to talk about options. I told her there was only one option for me and that was to keep the baby. She went right on talking as if she hadn't heard me, telling me about the many good families out here who wanted babies. Ans says I am not only ruining my own life but her son's as well. Judging from her attitude, it is clear she doesn't want me to have this baby. So in other words, she must want me to have an abortion. Never! I am determined to keep this baby and raise it on my own. J had an abortion and now regrets it. She said it was the worst decision she ever made. I wish Mike would step up to the plate, take responsibility for his child. I am hoping for a little girl. I am sick and weak all the time. The nurses say it is because of my pregnancy and it will pass. I hope they are right. I am going to need my health with a tiny baby depending on me.

Poor Mum, thought Zoë. It must have been awful being alone and pregnant. In the journals, her mother wrote about being sick and miserable most of the time. Sometimes she was so sick, she couldn't get out of bed. It warmed Zoë's heart that her mother loved her so much even before she was born, enduring sickness in order to have her. She finished the journal and picked up another. "Zoë smiled today for the first time. M. would have been so proud of her. Oh, what have I done? Poor M."

She stared at the elegant script. Poor M. *Mike?* Did her mother regret what she had done? If she felt so bad, why didn't she set things right?

Zoë lost all track of time. By the time she rowed back to shore, the sun was low, casting shadows. Mike was waiting for her on the beach. "Supper is almost ready, Zoë. What were you doing out there all this time? We were starting to worry."

"Sorry," she mumbled.

Mike put a steadying hand on her elbow as she got out of the boat. She saw that he had changed out of his jeans and was wearing white pants and a button-down shirt. Sarah didn't like them coming to the table in jeans if it was an important occasion like a birthday. Sometimes it got to be a pain, but Zoë was getting used to it.

While Mike pulled the boat up on the beach, she ran up the path to the cottage, taking off her grubby sneakers outside the door.

"Soo-prise," little Laura shouted when Zoë went inside. The walls were decorated with balloons, and there was a cake on the counter.

"Glad you could make it," Sarah said, smiling.

Zoë hurried upstairs and changed quickly into a denim skirt and red blouse.

When she returned, Mike, Sarah, and Laura were already seated around the table. Zoë took her place next to Laura's highchair. Only then did she realize the placemats, cups, and plates all matched. Sarah must have brought them from home; it bothered her when things were mismatched or out of place. Zoë had seen her arranging magazines in the dentist's office, straightening pictures in hotel lobbies. Still, she was touched that Sarah would go to so much trouble to make her birthday special. There were candles in fancy holders and flowers in vases. She even brought napkins with Zoë's name printed on them.

The chicken was crispy and tender, the rice done to perfection. The salad had fresh, crisp vegetables, and there were rolls hot from the oven.

After the main course, Mike brought out a large pink cake with "Happy Birthday Zoë" written in white icing. There were two candles, shaped like the numbers one and five, the kind you see on little kids' birthday cakes. Mike had put them together to make fifteen. He put the cake in front of Zoë, and the family sang "Happy Birthday."

"Make a wish," Sarah said.

"War-ah bow?" Laura asked, squirming to get closer.

"No, Laura," Sarah said firmly. "It's Zoë's cake."

"You can help," Zoë said. She closed her eyes, made a wish, then quickly blew out the candles.

Mike handed her a small package wrapped in silver paper. It was flat and square, the size of a cigarette package. "Open it," he urged, his voice eager.

She tore off the wrapping paper, uncovering a small black box. Inside was a picture taken with a Polaroid camera. A computer and printer set up on a computer desk. Baffled, Zoë turned the picture over in her hands while Mike and Sarah exchanged amused looks.

"Well?" Mike asked.

Zoë shrugged.

"It was too big to wrap and bring along."

"You got me a computer?"

"We figured it will come in handy with all your school assignments," Sarah said.

"Th…Thanks." Zoë wasn't used to expensive gifts. For Christmas and birthdays, Mum usually gave her something knitted or crocheted. Nearly every cent Mum earned went for food and rent. There was nothing left over for what she called non-essentials.

"Josh offered to help you learn how to use the software," Mike said. "He's good at computers."

Zoë smiled. Maybe her birthday wish would come true after all.

Sarah got up from the table, went to a sideboard, and fetched a red envelope. "I almost forgot," she said. "Opa brought this by on Friday while you were at school."

Inside, Zoë found a personalized card with letters embossed in gold calligraphy. "Granddaughter, Angels smiled when you were born." It had a picture of two smiling cherubs wrapping a ribbon around a large package. She opened it, and three scraps of paper fell into her plate. She picked them up, wiping away tomato sauce with a monogrammed napkin. "Tickets to *Twelfth Night*, the play Opa's directing," she said. "And a gift certificate for dinner for two at The Tempest." Even as she spoke, Zoë was making plans. She'd invite Josh to the play and take him to dinner afterwards as a way of thanking him for his help with her new computer software. She knew *Twelfth Night* was on the grade eleven reading list. Teachers tried to include plays they knew were going to be performed by Fathom Five.

There were still two unopened gifts on the table, one rectangular in shape, the other the size of a matchbox. Zoë reached for the smaller present and pulled away the envelope. Inside was a hand painted card from Ans. It simply read: "Love, Ans."

Without enthusiasm, Zoë untied the ribbon and pulled off the red foil wrapping. She found a purple crushed velvet box with "The Midas Touch" stamped in gold on the outside. Inside, was a dainty gold cross with a mini diamond in its centre.

"How lovely," Sarah exclaimed.

"Yes," Zoë agreed, but she snapped the box shut.

She could tell the last gift was a book even before she tore away the wrapping paper. The card said: "With love from Aunt Anneke, Uncle Mark, Andrew, and Erin." Zoë peeled away the paper and to her delight, found a book on art. She flipped through the glossy pages, marvelling at the colourful paintings and illustrations. There were chapters on how to use light, colour, and shadow effectively. On the cover was a print of the Mona Lisa. Recalling the lecture her art instructor had given on the painting, Zoë held up the book. "Look directly at her mouth, and tell me what you see," she said, glancing from Mike to Sarah.

"Umm. She's not smiling," Sarah said. "The Mona Lisa is not smiling."

"You're right," Mike said, squinting across the table. "The smile is gone."

"Now turn your gaze away from her mouth," Zoe instructed.

"Ahh," said Mike, "there's that famous smile."

"Interesting," Sarah said, "how we can look at the same image and see different things."

"Mum really enjoyed paintings like this one," Zoë said, and burst into tears.

Sarah looked uncomfortable. "Don't cry," she said. "There's no need to cry."

Awkwardly, Mike patted her shoulder. "It's only natural that you should miss your mother at a time like this, Zoë."

Laura spilled her milk. It ran down the leg of her chair and onto the hardwood floor. "I'll get it," Sarah said, moving quickly to mop up the mess.

CHAPTER 10: Josh

"My affections are most humble."
The Tempest

Zoë watched as Josh's mother made tea. She moved from the stove to the counter in a cotton skirt that came down past her knees. A solemn dark-eyed baby who looked like Josh clung to her hip, whimpering. The kitchen table was cluttered with books, papers, and magazines, the counter piled high with dishes, pots, and pans. *What's Josh doing?* she wondered. He had suggested she come to his house so he could show her how to use her new computer software, but had disappeared upstairs, leaving her in the kitchen with his mom and his cranky baby brother.

"What would you like in your tea, Zoë?"

"Just milk, Mrs. Carter."

"Call me Linda," she said. "Mrs. Carter makes me feel old." She smiled, and Zoë realized how pretty she was. Her eyes were the same colour as Josh's, and her hair was cut in a blunt, angled style that swung around her face. The baby started to cry, and she tried to comfort him by swaying her hips. "Ben's cutting his first-year molar," she explained. She moved some of the clutter away from the table and set down a jug of milk and a bowl of sugar.

Josh came downstairs. "It's all set up," he said. "Whenever you're ready."

"I've made tea for us, darling," Linda said. She handed him the baby. "Take Ben while I clear the table."

Zoë smiled. Most boys Josh's age would be horrified to be called darling by their mothers. But Josh didn't bat an eye.

Josh kissed the baby's head. "What's the matter, Bud?" he crooned. Linda moved books and magazines onto a chair to make room at the table. Two cats meandered into the kitchen and one of them jumped into Zoë's lap.

"Odeon, get down," Josh said.

"Oh, it's okay. I like cats. We can't have them at home because of Sarah allergies." She rubbed the cat's ears, and it purred loudly, rubbing its head against her.

"Josh tells me you're interested in the Maritime Archaic Indians." Linda poured tea into three mugs before taking baby Ben away from Josh.

"Yes. I'm working on a school project with Abbey Reid. We're both working at the site in Port au Choix for extra credit."

Linda nodded approvingly. "I keep telling Patty that the site is around the area where she is digging. It is only a matter of time before they find it." She added sugar to her tea. "I've become very interested in archaeology myself. In fact, I'm taking a correspondence course from Memorial University."

"It's all Leon's doing," Josh said.

"Leon?" Zoë looked from Josh to his mother.

"Leon Morgan is married to my cousin," Linda explained. "He teaches at MUN. During his visits to Port au Choix, he stays with us."

"Sarah teaches at MUN," Zoë said. "She probably knows Leon."

"She does," said Linda. "As a matter of fact, it was Leon who told her about the house for rent on our street. Anyway, Leon wrote a book, *Unlocking the Doors to the Past*. A great book." She took a sip of her tea. "I never thought archaeology could be so exciting."

"Nothing more thrilling than old bones." Josh winked at Zoë.

"It's about time people awoke to the importance of the past," Linda said defensively. "If we are to understand who we are, we must recognize our past."

Zoë knew Josh was only teasing. The morning he drove her to school, he seemed proud of the fact that his mother had an interest in archaeology.

The baby continued to fuss, and Linda unbuttoned her cotton blouse and placed her breast in his mouth. Embarrassed, Zoë averted her eyes. She glanced at Josh, but he seemed nonplussed, and she couldn't help thinking how different he was from the other boys she knew.

Josh sipped his tea and leaned back in his chair. The baby made gulping sounds at first, like someone starving, then the sucking became slow and rhythmic.

"Leon's giving a lecture the next time he comes here," Linda said. "Maybe you and Abbey would like to attend." The baby had stopped sucking now and had his eyes closed.

"That would be helpful," Zoë said. "I know Abbey would be interested. When is it?"

"I'm not sure, but I can let you know. It will probably be held at the museum."

Josh drained his cup and carried it to the sink. "Ready, Zoë?"

She gulped down the last of her tea, set her cup in the sink, and followed Josh up the carpeted stairs to a small bedroom with a sloping ceiling. She felt a little self-conscious going to a boy's bedroom. Josh's bed looked like it had been made in a hurry; sheets and blankets stuck out under the bedspread. *Did he tidy up because of me?* Zoë felt a flush creep up her neck, imagining him rushing around to make his room presentable for her. Still, he didn't do a very good job. There was a sock on the floor and his pyjama bottoms were flung on the bureau.

Josh switched on the computer, pulled up an extra chair, and gestured for Zoë to sit down. He opened the program and began explaining how it worked. He was so close, Zoë could smell the Ivory soap on his skin. With his arm resting on the back of her chair, brushing against her neck, she was finding it hard to concentrate. "Now, you try," he would say following each lesson. Her fingers felt clumsy on the keys, and she kept making mistakes. Josh had to show her everything twice. *He must think I'm some kind of dummy*, she thought. But Josh was a patient teacher who kept explaining everything until Zoë got it right.

"You've been ... very helpful," she stammered, then cleared her throat. "I have two tickets to see Fathom Five's production of *Twelfth Night*, and I was wondering ...," she swallowed, "... wondering if you'd be interested in going with me."

"Is it a date?" Josh asked bluntly.

"Well ... yes ... no ... yes," Zoë floundered. "What ...what I mean is ... the tickets are next Saturday. If that's not good, we can change them. To another time."

"Saturday's fine."

"You mean … you'll go with me?"

Josh held out an arm. It was tanned and muscled. "Pinch me," he said.

"Why?"

"Go ahead. Pinch me."

Feeling silly, Zoë gave his arm a small pinch.

"Ah, it's not a dream then," he said. "Here I am with this beautiful woman in my bedroom, and she has just asked me out on a date. Oh, come on. I must be dreaming." He began pinching his arm in an exaggerated way. "Wake up, Josh!"

Zoë was blushing like crazy. "I should go now," she said.

Josh walked her downstairs. Linda had put the baby to bed and was stacking dishes in the dishwasher. Zoë thanked her for the tea.

"You must come back again, Zoë," she said. "I really enjoyed our talk. I'll give you a call as soon as I find out more about the lecture."

"Thanks. I'll let Abbey know."

Outside, a group of little boys was playing street hockey. "She your girlfriend?" one of them asked.

Zoë hurried away, afraid of his answer.

CHAPTER 11: An Unexpected Find

"Alack, what trouble was I then to you?"
The Tempest

The next morning, Zoë was so tired she fell asleep in math class. Now she stifled a yawn as Ms. Robertson rambled about truth and illusion in Robert Browning's narrative poem, "The Ring and the Book." "The whole truth cannot be presented," she said, looking around the classroom. "It changes with each speaker."

How am I going to get through the day? Zoë wondered, closing her eyes. She had to be at the site this afternoon. Afterwards, they were going to Abbey's house to work on their project.

She thought about her meeting with Josh yesterday, the scene playing and replaying in her mind like a home movie. *A beautiful woman has just asked me for a date.* Had he really said that? It was the wee hours of the morning before she had been able to fall asleep. For most of the night, she had looked through the window. The moon was a perfect ripe apricot, making the night all silvery. The grey light of dawn was peeking in her window when she finally drifted off. This morning she had been so tired, it took all her energy just to get out of bed. "Wouldn't you agree, Zoë?" The voice seemed to be coming from far away. She opened her eyes, startled. Ms. Robertson was standing over her. "I *assume* you did the reading."

She shook her head, feeling herself flush. Titters came from the back of the classroom. Mercifully, the bell rang and kids began pushing books inside their backpacks. The teacher gave Zoë a sharp look before turning away.

Abbey came to stand by her desk, her bushy hair tamed neatly in a French braid. "We better go now," she said. "Matt won't wait if we're late, and I don't feel like walking all the way to Port au Choix."

Zoë stood up, shoved her books into her backpack. "I forgot your cousin was driving us," she said.

Abbey glanced at her watch. "He said he'd pick us up as soon as school got out. He has an appointment at the bank. Guess we'll have to eat our lunch on the way."

As they walked outside, Zoë told Abbey about her visit with Linda Carter. "Some professor is going to give a lecture on the Maritime Archaic Indians."

"Where at?"

"The museum, I think. Linda will let me know."

"There's Matt," Abbey said, as a red pickup truck pulled up in front of the school.

He let Zoë and Abbey off directly across the road from the site.

Monty, the site supervisor, greeted them with a warning. "Patty's not in a very good mood. She seems desperate, urging everyone to work faster, dig more holes."

Zoë nodded her understanding. She knew the pressure Patty was under and how difficult it was for her. Time was running out. Every day that went by without finding evidence of the habitation site, she became more dispirited. The team now dug even in rainy and foggy weather.

Abbey looked toward the woods where Dora's son, Jimmy, and Bonnie Humby were digging. "Since when did we start using shovels?" she asked.

Monty shook his head. "I know, I know," he said. "Not the proper way to dig up an archaeological site, but we don't have time to use trowels."

Abbey's mouth tightened. "Is that what it has come to?"

They were walking to their trenches when a rock went flying through the air.

"Hold it," Monty shouted to the diggers. "Hold it, you guys!"

Bonnie and Jimmy put down their shovels.

Monty picked up the rock and studied it. Zoë could see it had a pinkish hue, but she couldn't imagine what value it would have.

Monty picked up a trowel and jumped down in the pit. "What is it?" Zoë asked.

Monty didn't answer right away; he was too busy scraping away peat with his trowel. After some time, a ring of rocks emerged. "A hearth," he said, breathlessly. "We've uncovered a hearth."

Zoë's heart leapt. "Does that mean we found the habitation site?"

"No," Monty answered. "It may not even be Maritime Archaic. It could be recent Indian."

"You mean Beothuk?"

"Possibly."

Zoë knew Beothuk Indians lived in Newfoundland at the time of European contact. But there was no direct evidence they had ever lived in Port au Choix.

"Wow, wouldn't it be cool if this belonged to the Beothuk," Abbey said.

Monty nodded. "I can't wait to show it to Patty, to see what she thinks."

Monty turned to Bonnie and Jimmy. "Okay you guys, no more shovels. We have to go back to using trowels."

Zoë and Abbey got a ride home with Jessie and her mother, who let them off at the entrance to the subdivision. As they were walking pass Josh's house, Zoë saw him in the driveway with a girl—a very pretty girl she thought, taking in the black hair that came down past her shoulders. The girl turned her head, smiling up at Josh, a cleft in her chin adding to her beauty. She said something that made Josh laugh. He put his arm around her, pulling her to his chest. Zoë turned her head. Abbey, who had been chattering a mile a minute, didn't seem to notice Josh and the girl.

Abbey's parents were both at work, so she and Zoë had the house to themselves. After hanging their coats in the closet, Abbey led Zoë into the dining room. A file folder was open on table, along with brochures, the kind you see in tourist bureaus. "Millie at the museum gave them to me," Abbey said.

The focus of the project was to show how art played a role in the life of the Maritime Archaic Indians. From visits to the museum, Zoë knew they decorated their clothing with rows of seal claws and small bone pendants. Shell beads and other ornaments were sewn onto clothing, sealskin pouches, and moccasins. Much of their art focused on seals, birds, and whales.

Abbey opened a brochure that had colourful pictures of carved pendants shaped like bears, birds, and humans. "These objects were not only valued for their beauty but for their supernatural powers," she read.

Zoë nodded, but her mind was not on the project. She was thinking of Josh and the girl.

"They were intended to ensure success in hunting," Abbey continued. "By carving an image of a bear or a whale, the hunter hoped to gain the strength of that animal."

"We could make a jacket and decorate it with shells and beads the way the Maritime Archaic Indians did," Zoë suggested. "I'm good at sewing."

"Great idea. I'll find shells and beads to sew on." Abbey gave her a wide smile. "Mr. Bean will be impressed, I'm sure."

It was nearly five by the time Zoë left Abbey's. Dora was in the kitchen preparing supper, watching Oprah Winfrey on a small television as she worked.

"Would you like some help?" Zoë asked.

"No, my love, the meal's almost done." She gestured to the television where a man and woman were arguing. "She's got them all fired up again today."

"Yes," Zoë said absently. "If you need me, I'll be in the basement." She went downstairs where Mike had set up a small room for her to use as a studio. She had been copying a still life titled *Strawberry Tart Supreme*. Her instructor often had them copy works by famous artists. *I have a long way to go,* Zoe thought as she compared the two paintings. In the original, the chocolate icing and strawberries looked so real, she had an urge to lick the canvas. Her own version lacked the depth that gave the illusion of reality. *Maybe I should stick with landscapes*, she thought. After nearly twenty minutes of working on the painting, trying to give it dimension, she gave up and went back upstairs. She couldn't get her mind off Josh and the girl. Who was she? It wasn't anyone she knew from school.

Zoë went to her room and took out the newest journals Aunt Caroline had sent. She flipped through the pages scanning poems, songs, and quotations written in her mother's elaborate script. Most of the entries were not dated. The accounts Zoë liked best were those written about her when she was little. Near the end of the book, she came across an entry dated February 1982. Eagerly, she began to read, but the words stopped her cold: "I am scheduled for an abortion next week. I never thought I would do something like this, but I know in my heart I can't have this child. The doctor explained the procedure to me, but I was only half listening. I don't want to know all the gory details. In another week this will be over and I'll be free."

"An abortion," Zoë whispered, the room spinning around her. Obviously, Mum didn't go through with it. Still, she couldn't shake the feeling of disquiet that had settled over her like a damp blanket. Shivering, she wrapped her arms around her knees, pulling herself into a tight, protective ball. Had Mum thought of *aborting* her?

CHAPTER 12: Searching for the Truth

"The strangeness of your story put heaviness in me."
The Tempest

"I've already put a couple of your mother's journals in the mail," Aunt Caroline told Zoë over the phone the following day. "They should have arrived by now."

"I didn't get them yet," she said. "But I'll check the post office on Monday."

"I'm glad your mother's journals are giving you some comfort, Zoë."

Comfort wasn't exactly the word Zoë would have used, but she said nothing.

"I'll tell Amber you called," Aunt Caroline said. "Too bad she's out."

"Thanks, Aunt Caroline. Bye."

"You take care, sweetie."

Zoë put down the receiver. Maybe the new journals would shed light on what her mother had written. She desperately needed to get this matter cleared up. Last night she had lain awake, thinking of possible explanations for what her mother had written. The worst scenario she could imagine was that her mother wanted an abortion, but for some reason wasn't able to get one. *The important thing is that she didn't have the abortion*, Zoë firmly reminded herself in an attempt to banish the disturbing thought from her mind. She had a date with Josh this evening, and she wasn't going to ruin it by fretting about what she had read in the journal.

Glancing at her watch, she saw it was nearly seven. Josh would be arriving any minute now to take her to the theatre. Mike, Sarah, and Laura were at the airport picking up Sarah's parents who were spending the week with them.

Studying herself in the full-length mirror, Zoë wondered if her new black jeans with the wide belt were suitable for the theatre. Not a theatre really, she reminded herself. The company performed in a church hall.

It was quarter past seven when Josh rang the doorbell. He was wearing blue jeans and a white shirt under a blue V-neck sweater. She noticed his hair had been trimmed. He waved a set of car keys. "I borrowed Dad's car. Better than my own rust heap."

"I'm ready," Zoë said, reaching for her coat.

The small foyer was crowded. Students had come from up and down the coast. Zoë knew they were there to fill a course requirement. Shakespeare was not very popular with people her own age. She looked at the framed reviews and photographs of actors and actresses posted on the walls. Opa smiled down from his place of honour. "Alexander van der Post, Artistic Director," was written below his photograph. Zoë felt a surge of pride as she read reviews from the *Northern Pen* and the *Humber Log*. There was an article on the actress who was playing Viola. "She's a close friend of Opa's," Zoë told Josh. "She came from Halifax to be in his play."

"Must be a special lady."

Zoë nodded. "Opa says he's lucky to get her."

An usher took their tickets and led them toward a row of wooden chairs near the front. While they waited for the play to begin, Josh entertained her with stories about his brothers, Roger and Glenn, the six-year-old twins.

"They're so bad, poor Mom goes around pulling her hair out."

"I've never had a brother or sister," Zoë said. "I didn't even know about Laura until a few months ago. Now Sarah's pregnant."

The lights went down and a hush fell over the audience. A streak of lightening lit up the stage, followed by a loud clap of thunder. There were gasps of surprise from the audience.

Josh leaned forward, and Zoë noticed a smile on his lips as he watched the drama of the storm play out at sea. Viola and her twin brother, Sebastian, become separated during a shipwreck. Each believing the other has drowned, they each set out on their own. Viola disguises herself as a boy and, looking identical to her twin brother, poses as a page in the household of the Duke. Throughout the play, characters are not who they appear to be and this causes much misunderstanding and confusion. Olivia, a rich noblewoman, falls in love with the disguised Viola. Viola, on the other hand, falls for the Duke. The comic mix-ups that come about because of the mistaken identities were so funny that Zoë laughed out loud. For a while she was able to forget what she had read in her mother's journal, yet it still lurked at the back of her mind like a wild animal ready to pounce when least expected.

The lights went down, signalling the end of the third act and the beginning of intermission. They went out to the lobby where Josh ordered Cokes at the bar.

"Your grandfather did a good job," he told Zoë. "The thunder and lightning was brilliant. How did he create such an illusion?"

Zoë nodded. "I'm still trying to figure that out."

"The play's great too," Josh said. "You know, here in Newfoundland, we celebrate the twelve days of Christmas just like in Shakespeare's day."

"Really?"

Josh nodded. "The 'twelfth night' here is January sixth. Old Christmas Day, we call it. Back when my parents were young there used to be mummers all during Christmas. Not so many now. But we do go out now and then."

"Mummers?" Zoë had never heard of such a thing.

"People in the community who disguise themselves in costumes. They cover their faces with masks or veils and go door to door during the twelve days of Christmas, entertaining people with songs and music."

"That's really cool," Zoë said.

The bell rang, signalling the end of intermission, and Josh and Zoë went back inside the theatre.

All through the fourth and fifth acts, Zoë found herself gazing sideways at Josh. He had stretched his arm across the back of her chair so that his fingers were lightly touching her neck and shoulder. Would he ever invite her out? She thought of the girl she'd seen him with while she was walking past his house. Was she Josh's girlfriend?

Instead of going directly to the restaurant after the play, Josh took Zoë for a walk along the shore. He held her hand, and she wished the night would go on forever.

By the time they got to The Tempest, the place was crowded. The cast of the play sat at a long table at the back of the restaurant. Their shouted conversations were already starting to get a little rowdy. Zoë scanned the crowd looking for Opa, but he was not among them. A little man with bow legs and buckteeth led them to a table by the big window overlooking the water.

"That's Caliban," Zoë whispered. "The monster from Shakespeare's play."

"I love coming here," Josh said, after they were seated. "About time someone opened a restaurant around here. But who would've thought there'd be a place like this? It's so amazing."

"I agree," Zoë said, taking in the waiters and waitresses in their elaborate costumes. The place was even more beautiful at night. Every table had a red linen cloth with matching napkins. There were lanterns with lighted candles inside.

"There was an article in *Maclean's* magazine about this restaurant," Josh said. "The author talked about your grandfather's brilliant ideas."

"He's wonderful," Zoë agreed, a note of pride in her voice.

"O' brave new world."

Zoë looked up from her menu at the waitress who had come to take their orders. It was the same girl who had come into the bathroom to fetch Zoë the day Opa took her to lunch. She was wearing the same blue dress with sequins down the front. Bits of coloured glass and jewellery clung to her black hair.

"Darlene?" Josh said, sounding surprised.

"Miranda," the waitress corrected. "Call me Miranda."

"Miranda, is it?"

She laughed. "The manager says we should keep things as authentic as possible."

"I see," Josh said, playing along. "Miranda, this is my friend Zoë."

"Welcome to my island," the girl said. If she remembered Zoë from when she was there with Opa, she didn't let on.

"Dar ... um ... Miranda and I used to sleep together."

The waitress hit him with the menu.

"In Mr. Flynn's grade nine English class," Josh added when he saw Zoë's startled look.

Miranda laughed, showing perfect white teeth. Everything about her sparkled—her hair, eyes, teeth, everything.

"What qualifications do you need to work here?" Josh asked.

Miranda smiled at him. "Are you interested?"

"As long as I don't have to look too foolish." Josh glanced at one of the waiters who was wearing purple leotards and shoes with pointed toes.

"Most of the people who work here are drama students," Miranda explained. "But it's not a requirement." She lowered her voice confidentially. "Actually, we're looking for a part-time Ferdinand. One of our Ferdinands quit yesterday." She smiled sweetly at Josh. "If you like, I'll put in a good word for you."

"Sure." Josh squeezed her arm.

Cute, Zoë thought. *Miranda and Ferdinand.*

"So what will it be?" Miranda pulled a pen and pad from the folds of her costume.

"What do you recommend, Madame?" Josh asked.

"The lasagne is very good."

"I had it the last time I was here," Zoë cut in.

"It's our most popular dish," Miranda said.

"Sounds good." Josh looked at Zoë.

"Make it two lasagnes," she said, realizing it was her treat. "Anything else, Josh?"

Josh closed the menu and handed it to Miranda. "An order of garlic bread."

Miranda wrote it on her pad and moved on to the next table.

Josh tried to tell Zoë about the fun they'd had in Mr. Flynn's English class, but Zoë quickly changed the subject. "I'd like to paint that sometime," she said, gesturing to the scene outside the window.

"It *is* pretty," said Josh. He met her gaze. "I've always admired people who can draw and paint. Maybe because I've always found it so difficult." He laughed. "The only thing I've ever painted came in a paint-by-numbers kit."

Zoë told him about the art workshop she took in Toronto. "After that, I wanted to do nothing else but paint."

At the piano, Ariel was singing:

"Full fathom five thy father lies; of his bones are coral made those are pearls that were his eyes."

"I'm so tired of hearing that song sung over and over," Miranda said, returning with their orders. "When I get home, I hear it in my head." She left them alone after that, stopping by their table only to bring drinks or take away dishes.

Long after they'd eaten, Josh and Zoë lingered at the restaurant, sipping hot chocolate and talking. By now, most of the customers had left. Josh asked Zoë about her work on the site. She told him how she had become interested in prehistoric peoples. He told her about his plans to go to veterinary college someday.

"I gather you really like animals," Zoë said, recalling his numerous cats and all the times she saw him walking his neighbour's dog.

Josh nodded. "I love all animals, but cats are my favourite."

It was nearly midnight by the time Josh pulled the car into their street. "I had a really good time this evening, Zoë," he said. "Next weekend is movie night at the library in Daniel's Harbour. I'm planning to drive down there. Would you like to come with me?"

"Y-yes. I'd like that."

"Good." Josh smiled at her. "I'll pick you up Friday around six thirty."

At that moment Mike's van drove into the driveway.

"Sarah's parents' flight must have been delayed," Zoë said. She reached for the door handle. "I'll see you at school, Josh."

"Goodbye, Zoë," he said, then drove off.

Sarah got out of the van, Laura resting against her shoulder. Mike emerged from the driver's side and opened the side door to let Sarah's parents out.

"Zoë," Mike called. "Come meet Charles and Monika."

Zoë walked toward them. Monika was a tiny woman who appeared nervous and self-conscious. Charles, in contrast, looked like he was going to burst out of his grey suit. He bore only the slightest resemblance to the portrait of him that hung in the dining room.

"This is my daughter, Zoë," Mike said. "Zoë, meet Sarah's parents, Charles and Monika."

"Hello," Monika said shyly.

Charles squeezed her hand with a beefy paw. "So you're the girl my son-in-law's been hiding," he said loudly.

Mike shot him a sharp look.

"Pleased to meet you," Zoë mumbled.

Charles picked up a suitcase and headed toward the house, Monika in tow.

Zoë thought of Charles's portrait. "What happened to Sarah's dad?" she whispered to Mike. "He's gained about a hundred pounds and lost most of his hair."

"Not at all." Mike grinned and winked. "He had the artist paint him that way."

CHAPTER 13: A Stunning Revelation

"What foul play had we that we came from thence?"
The Tempest

Aunt Caroline's parcel had been put in Mike's study by mistake. "It came two days ago," Sarah had said when she handed it to Zoë this morning. Zoë had eagerly torn off the wrapping to find two more of Mum's journals, but she'd been kept busy all morning, helping Sarah prepare dinner and hadn't had a chance to read them. The comment about Mum wanting an abortion had to be no more than a fleeting thought, she told herself now as she polished the silver. Still, her stomach churned whenever she thought about it.

To keep her mind off the journals, Zoë mentally counted the people who would be at dinner. Ans and Opa were coming, along with Sarah's parents who were still upstairs. There would be eight of them, including Laura.

Sarah had already put the roast in the oven, and a mouthwatering aroma drifted from the kitchen. Zoë finished polishing the silverware and went to help her peel vegetables.

"Sarah, have you seen Laura's Beanie Baby?" Mike called from the living room. "She won't go for a nap without it."

Sarah wiped her hands on her apron and went into the living room. She looked in the space between the sofa and coffee table, retrieved the lost Beanie, and handed it to Mike.

"Aren't you a little old to be playing with dolls?" The voice came from the top of the stairs. Sarah's dad gave a raspy laugh, his gold tooth glinting.

"Good morning, Charles," Mike called.

Charles slowly walked downstairs, panting from exertion.

"By Jove that roast smells good," he said, sniffing the air. "When will dinner be ready?"

"It's only eleven thirty, Daddy," Sarah said. "Dinner's not until one."

"Jolly good. I'll have time to make a sandwich before lunch."

Ans was the first to arrive, Opa moments later, carrying four red roses. "For my ladies," he said. When he handed Ans her flower, he kissed her cheek.

Sarah had put out her best china, delicate plates and cups decorated with little roses. Cut glass vases held fresh flowers. There were candles in elegant holders and lace napkins folded into long-stemmed water glasses. *The dining room table looks like something out of Better Homes and Gardens,* Zoë thought, recalling the magazines Mum brought home from houses she cleaned.

"Looks like you've been working hard, dear," Ans said after they were seated. She gazed the length of the table, taking in the assortment of vegetables, the silver and glass bowls containing various salads, rice, and dressings. "Remember your condition."

"Not too long now before our grandson arrives," Charles said.

"Or granddaughter," Monika said, her voice barely audible. "I wouldn't mind having another granddaughter."

"The baby's not due until March," Sarah reminded them. She was wearing a pink maternity top and black pants. She placed her hand gently on her stomach where the baby was just starting to grow.

"Bet Mike would like a son," Charles said.

Mike merely shrugged.

Zoë looked from Mike to Sarah. She had noticed that whenever the subject of the baby came up, Mike got quiet. Could there be something wrong with Sarah's baby? But Sarah was always happy to talk about her pregnancy. Surely she would know if there was a problem.

"Charles," Mike said. "Would you say the blessing?"

Charles bowed his head and closed his eyes. "Thank you, Lord, for our food, and may we continue to prosper. Amen."

"Amen," everyone echoed.

"You're a wonderful cook, my dear," Opa said graciously.

There were murmurs of agreement around the table. Sarah beamed, obviously pleased.

Opa peered across the table at Zoë. "Zoë and a schoolmate are doing a project on the Maritime Archaic Indians," he said.

Everyone's attention was on Zoë now.

"It's for social studies class," she explained. "We're making a jacket decorated with shells and beads."

"I gave her some leather that was used for props at the theatre," Opa said.

"Interesting," Charles said. "Interesting indeed." But it was clear to Zoë that he couldn't care less about her project.

Mike launched into a discussion about how unfairly doctors were treated in Canada. Many of his friends, who had moved to the United States, were making nearly twice as much money. Canadian doctors were just not appreciated.

Sarah got up to clear away the dishes. "I'll do it," Zoë offered and before Sarah could answer, began clearing the table.

For dessert, Sarah served a chocolate trifle with cherries on top. "This will probably kill Daddy," she said.

"Nah," said Charles, "a few calories never hurt anyone."

That started Mike on another tirade about new evidence that linked cholesterol to heart failure.

Zoë stifled a yawn. She had to get away from the table. Not only was the conversation boring, but she was eager to begin reading the journals. "May I be excused?" she asked.

"You haven't eaten your dessert," Sarah said.

"I have a lot of homework."

Sarah nodded.

Zoë left the table and hurried upstairs. With trembling hands, she took the journals from the box. She turned the pages with a feeling of anxiety. What evidence would she uncover today? Did she really want to discover anything new?

The first journal was filled with poetry and inspirational quotes from poets, artists, and philosophers. Zoë read for twenty minutes, but couldn't find anything pertaining to the earlier journal. There was no mention of her mother's pregnancy at all. She picked up the second journal and opened the cover. On the first page there was only one sentence: "It is finished."

Zoë stared hard at the three words, her mind trying to absorb what it all meant. Baffled, she pulled out the previous journal and read the words again. "I am scheduled for an abortion next week. I never thought I would do something like this, but I know in my heart I can't have this child. The doctor explained the procedure to me, but I was only half listening. I don't want to know all the gory details. In another week all of this will be over and I will be free." The words made no more sense now than they did a few days ago.

She turned back to the present journal and continued to read. There were pages filled with poetry. Many of the poems were about death. One was about a gift, carelessly thrown away. A gift that could have brought the receiver "joy, love, and happiness."

Zoë slowly turned the thin pages, trying to make sense of it all. Toward the end of the journal, she found an entry that made her heart stop. "I knew it would not be easy," she read, "but nothing could prepare me for this. The doctor told me that after the abortion I would have a hollow feeling as if I had been scooped out. It feels as if my heart has been scooped away, and I am left with this empty feeling that can never be filled. How do I get over this?"

CHAPTER 14: Betrayed

"Sweet lord you play me false."
The Tempest

The following Friday afternoon, Abbey's mother drove Zoë and Abbey to Port au Choix and let them off near the Pointe Riche lighthouse. Today they were going to dig in Phillip's Garden, a new experience.

"It's going to be so much more interesting at this site," Abbey said as they walked along the rocky shore. "Much prettier too."

Zoë nodded. Phillip's Garden looked out over the ocean, and she could hear the roar of the waves and the cry of gulls.

Abbey gestured toward the ocean. "We often see whales and icebergs from here."

Zoë was barely listening. Her mind was on what she had read in her mother's journals. As much as she tried to shake it from her mind, all week long she thought of little else. It had become an obsession, and it was difficult to concentrate on anything else.

As they neared the site, she saw that Jessie had already arrived. She and Patty were standing near the shallow trenches. "Hi girls," Patty called when she saw them. There were about a dozen other diggers, all busy with trowels and brushes.

"Hi yourself," Zoë called as she set down her backpack.

"I was just telling Jessie that this is going to be a whole different experience than the Loyal site," Patty said. "For one thing, this area is much richer in artifacts."

"So I heard," Zoë replied. She knew Patty wanted them to continue digging at the Loyal site. Time was running out and they were frantically searching for the Maritime Archaic habitation site. But there was an agreement with the school that students would be given an opportunity to work at various sites. Mr. Bean said it was to broaden their knowledge about all the prehistoric cultures in the area.

"I'm expected back at the Loyal site," Patty said, checking her watch. "Alexis will tell you a little about the history here." Zoë also knew that it was in the agreement that the archaeologists explain the different cultures that had occupied the various sites. She glanced at a woman a few feet away with a blue kerchief tied around her head. She was explaining something to one of the team members. Zoë remembered Alexis from the first day she came to the site with Sarah.

A few minutes passed before Alexis was available. "Welcome," she said as she approached. "I love seeing young people so involved. I'm Alexis, by the way."

Each of the girls introduced herself in turn.

"We refer to this site as Phillip's Garden East," Alexis said. "It's the richest of the five Groswater Palaeoeskimo sites in the area. Groswater people lived here between 2,800 and 2,200 years ago. Once you start digging, you'll find a lot of well-preserved animal bone, especially seal." She paused to take a swallow of water from a bottle. "Seals would have been plentiful, arriving in early spring." She nodded toward the ocean. "Even today, it's a good spot to set out for seals."

"At least they wouldn't have gone hungry," Abbey said.

"Seals, like most other animals, would have been a valuable food source," Alexis agreed, "but they had other value. Sealskins would have been used for clothing and tent covering. Seal oil would have been used for fuel and the bones to make various tools."

Alexis talked at length about the various animals in the area and their value to the Groswater. Although Zoë nodded politely, she was impatient, itching to start digging.

"If you have any questions," Alexis said, wrapping up her talk, "I'll be available."

Zoë had been digging only a few minutes when she found a whalebone. In less than an hour, she had piles of bones from various animals. *Alexis is right,* she thought. *There's no end to the bones here.*

Half an hour later, Sarah dropped by. Zoë had expected to see a lot of her stepmother after she signed on at the site. But like an apparition, Sarah could appear and disappear at a moment's notice. "Hi Zoë," she called cheerfully.

Zoë waved at her from her trench.

Sarah stopped to talk with Alexis, and Zoë went back to her digging. She would have liked to be able to confide in Sarah about what she had read in her mother's journals, but she did not have that kind of relationship with her stepmother. Maybe she never would.

After a while, Zoë came across a strange looking rock. It resembled a small coconut and had a deep crack down one side.

Sarah had come over to see how things were going. "That's a fire-cracked rock," she explained. "We find them throughout the site."

"They're cracked and discoloured because they've been placed in a fire," Abbey said.

Sarah smiled and nodded, obviously pleased with Abbey's knowledge. "They were used to heat liquids or to spread heat throughout a lodging," she explained, running her finger along the rock.

"Oh my God!" Jessie shrieked. "Oh my God! Alexis come see!"

"Jessie must have found another rock," Abbey said.

"It's not a rock," Jessie said, indignantly. She held out her hand. Resting on her palm was a sharp pointed stone, triangular in shape.

"That's a side-blade," Alexis explained. "Used by the Paleoeskimo. Among other uses, they were slotted into bone handles to make knives."

"Cool!" said Zoë. She looked around for Sarah, but she had already left the site.

The afternoon passed quickly. Zoë found a ton of bones, more fire-cracked rocks, even a scraper. She was so absorbed in her treasures she had little time to think about what she had read in her mother's journals. Aunt Caroline once said that after a woman gives birth, her hormones get all out of whack. She used to joke about how she had insisted little Paul was not her baby. Could Mum have had some kind of breakdown? *I'm not going to worry about it anymore*, she thought, trying to banish the uneasiness from her mind. She had a date with Josh tonight, and she wasn't going to let anything spoil it.

Zoë looked out the living room window toward Josh's house. His brothers were playing hockey with nets set up on the street. A tangle of hockey sticks, bicycles, roller skates, and baseballs littered the driveway and front lawn. She could hear Roger yelling. Josh once told her that neighbours sometimes complained about all the noise his brothers made. She was about to turn away from the window when she caught sight of Josh and a girl—the same girl he was with the day Zoë walked to Abbey's house. She watched them walk down the driveway to Josh's car, which was parked on the street.

"Where are you taking Madeline?" Roger called in his high-pitched voice.

Josh said something she couldn't make out.

"Doe-e?"

Zoë turned to see Laura, who had wandered downstairs from the nursery. Sarah had asked Zoë to keep an eye on her while Mike worked in his study. Sarah's parents had gone home after a week's visit, and both Sarah and Mike had a lot of work to catch up on.

"War-ah see Daddy," Laura said.

"C'mon Laura," Zoë said, closing the window. "Let's see if we can find something to do."

"War-ah see Daddy," she insisted. And before Zoë could stop her, she ran across the hall to Mike's study, opened the door, and rushed in.

"Sorry," Zoë mumbled, going after her.

Laura grabbed a plastic model of a fetus from Mike's desk. "Be-be."

"Give Daddy the baby," Mike said, prying it from her tiny fist. "It's very fragile. We wouldn't want it to break, would we?"

Zoë looked around his office. Framed diplomas hung on the walls, along with diagrams of uteruses and ovaries. There were posters of fetuses in various stages of development. Along one wall were shelves stacked with books: *New Hope for the Infertile Couple*, *Getting Pregnant After Forty*, and *Endometriosis*.

Mike took a shiny poster of a baby from his drawer and gave it to Laura. "NURTURE: The next best thing to mother's breast" was written across the top. "Here's a baby for Laura," he said.

"You'll soon have a baby brother or sister of your own." Zoë glanced quickly at Mike.

A shadow fell across his face, but he said nothing. Again she wondered if there was something wrong with Sarah's baby.

Pleased with her baby, Laura let Zoë take her hand and lead her to the nursery. She sat at her little table and scribbled on the baby's face with a red crayon. "Pretty," she said, proudly showing Zoë her work. "Be-be pretty."

"You've ruined it," Zoë said. As soon as the words left her mouth she was sorry. She realized she couldn't expect a two-year-old to know any better. Still, it was disturbing to see the baby's destroyed face.

Laura gave her a blank stare and continued to scribble. Zoë ruffled her hair and smiled in spite of everything. Laura looked so cute in her Raggedy Ann dress, red curls framing her chubby face.

Laura quickly lost interest in the picture, and Zoë gazed around the room looking for something else to involve her in. Laura's room was like a toy store with shelves filled with books, games, and puzzles. Dozens of stuffed animals sat on shelves and bureaus. In one corner was a dollhouse big enough for Laura to walk inside.

Zoë searched for paint and glue, but couldn't find any. Maybe Sarah was afraid Laura would get messy. Zoë used to help her mother at the day care. The kids loved working with paste and fingerpaint. Sometimes they made collage men, using buttons and beads and pearls for eyes.

Laura went to her bookshelf and picked out *Are you my mother?* by P. D. Eastman. "Read," she said, climbing onto Zoë's lap. Zoë read the story about a baby bird that hatches while his mother is away from the nest. The bird wanders all over the place, looking for her. "Are you my mother?" he asks every creature he meets.

"You muffer?" Laura repeated after Zoë.

Zoë finished the book, and Laura went to get another: A brightly illustrated copy of Cinderella. Somewhere between Cinderella dancing with the prince and leaving the ball, Laura fell asleep. Zoë carried her to her little pink bed, covered her with a quilt, and quietly left the room.

In her own room, she sat quietly on her bed, brooding about Josh. *Why shouldn't I care?* she reasoned. *Josh is taking me out tonight.*

She went to the closet and took out her mother's journals, which she had not looked at since Sarah's dinner party last weekend. She was afraid of what else she might find.

There must be some explanation for what Mum wrote, Zoë told herself now, as she turned the pages of the journal. The first few entries were written shortly after her birth. Her mother had recorded her first smile, first tooth, when she first started to crawl.

She read for another half an hour, and then she came across something that made her blood run cold. "No," she whispered.

She reread the entry, the words running together on the page. *My God. That can't be true. It just can't be true.* She closed the journal, her heart pounding. Wrapping her arms around her legs, she rested her forehead on her knees. She felt like she did the time she fell off a slide in first grade and had the wind knocked out of her. She had recovered quickly from her fall, but could she recover from the shock of the truth she had just learned?

To keep her mind off what she'd read in the journals and to fill time while she waited for Josh, Zoë helped Sarah and Mike address invitations for their eighth anniversary. To celebrate, they were planning a party at The Tempest. It was past seven when the doorbell rang. Josh was over half an hour late.

"Sorry," he apologized when Zoë opened the door.

A thousand questions came to her mind. "What happened?" she asked.

"I got the job at the restaurant," he said cheerfully as he stepped inside. "I start tomorrow evening."

"Congratulations. Are you the new Ferdinand?"

"Actually, I've been hired as a floating character."

Zoë stared at him.

"Whenever a character can't make it to work, I get to play his part," Josh went on to explain.

"Cool."

"I have to dress in weird costumes, but the pay's decent and the tips are good."

"Thought you said your interview was at four o'clock."

"Yes. I ... umm ... took my aunt out to help me celebrate."

He's lying to me, Zoë thought, her heart sinking. She wanted to ask him about Madeline, the girl he was with earlier, but silently she went to get her coat from the closet. "We better leave now if we want to make it to the movie on time."

Zoë couldn't concentrate on the movie; her thoughts kept flashing back to the entry she'd just read in her mother's journal. She felt betrayed. Betrayed by her mother. Betrayed by Josh. Why did people lie to her? She stole a glance at Josh's lean, handsome face. He caught her looking at him and reached out to squeeze her hand.

"Would you like to go to The Tempest for coffee?" he asked her after the film.

"I'd rather go for a drive," she said. The last thing she needed was to be around Darlene with her smiles and silks and sequins.

"Let's drive down the coast," Josh said, taking her hand and leading her to the car.

They drove in silence, the ocean on one side of them, the light of a full moon shining down on the dark sea. She could hear waves crashing against the shore.

After some time, Josh turned onto a gravel road and drove onto a long wharf. The moon made a golden path of light on the black water, and the sound of the ocean was all around them. For a long time they sat breathing in the moist salt air. Zoë's thoughts were on what she had read in her mother's journal. When Josh put an arm around her, she pulled away abruptly.

"Are you okay?"

Zoë didn't answer. She was trembling and close to tears.

"It's still early," Josh said. "If you like, we could still go to The Tempest. Darlene is working this evening. I saw her earlier when I took my aunt there to celebrate."

Anger swelled up inside Zoë. Why did he keep lying?

"If you wanted to be with Darlene, you should have invited her out instead of me." The words were out before she could stop them.

Josh raised an eyebrow. "Sounds like you might be jealous," he teased.

"I'm not jealous," she said, with further irritation. "I'm sick and tired of you lying to me."

A heavy silence followed. Josh turned to her, a stunned look on his face. "I've never lied to you, Zoë," he said in a quiet, even voice.

The moon drifted behind a cloud, and a menacing darkness spread over the water. Zoë shivered, wishing she could take back her words. But he *had* lied.

Without another word, Josh started the car. They drove home in silence, and when they pulled up in front of Zoë's house, Josh stopped abruptly, making the tires squeal. He sat stiffly, both hands gripping the steering wheel, his jaw set in a grim line. He didn't even look at her as she got out of the car.

The moon cast gloomy shadows on the side of the house. Somewhere, a shed door was banging. Zoë hurried up the driveway as Josh drove away.

CHAPTER 15: An Unexpected Gift

"With eyes wide open; standing, speaking, moving,
and yet so fast asleep."
The Tempest

Zoë couldn't remember how she came to be in the bathroom or why she was standing in a puddle of water. Her mother's journal was on the floor, wet pages floating around her ankles. Mike and Sarah stood in the doorway. "What in heaven's name is she doing?" Sarah whispered.

"Careful," Mike cautioned. "She's asleep. We don't want to startle her."

But Zoë was fully awake now. She discovered she had been trying to flush her mother's journal down the toilet.

"Zoë?" Mike quietly took her elbow and steered her out of the bathroom. "Better get some towels to soak up the water," he told Sarah. "We may have to call a plumber in the morning." Without another word, he led Zoë to her room.

"I didn't mean …"

"It's okay," he said quietly.

Zoë climbed into bed, the hems of her pyjama legs still wet. Mike tucked a thick warm blanket around her. "Try to get some sleep." He left the room, closing the door softly.

She fell into an exhausted sleep but awoke a few hours later, feeling troubled and frightened. Mum's journals were on her night table, bits of torn paper clinging to the spirals. The events of the night before came surging back. She recalled the fight with Josh, the incident in the bathroom. Wearily, she got out of bed, dressed quickly, and went downstairs.

"Hi, Doe-e." Laura greeted her at the bottom of the steps. She had a sippy cup in one hand, a teddy bear dangling from the other. Zoë gave her a quick hug before going into the kitchen.

Sarah was frying eggs inside two metal circles so they would be round and perfect. "There are pancakes and sausage," she said. "The eggs are almost ready." She didn't mention last night.

"Thanks, but I'm not hungry. I think I'll go for a walk."

Sarah handed her a bundle of stamped envelopes, the invitations for the anniversary party. "Would you mind dropping these in the mailbox?"

Zoë took the envelopes and went to get her jacket from the closet.

It was cold for late September, and Zoë's breath rose like smoke. She walked briskly past Josh's house, trying not to think of what happened between them last night.

Again, her thoughts turned to what she had read in her mother's journal. Mike and Sarah would have to know the truth. How was she going to break the news to them?

"Zoë!"

She turned to see Linda Carter pushing baby Ben in his stroller. Zoë stifled a groan. Josh's mother was the last person she wanted to see right now. But she stopped and politely waited for her to catch up.

"I've been wanting to talk with you," Linda said, sounding out of breath. "As a matter of fact, I was going to call you today."

"Call me." Zoë echoed dumbly. Did Josh tell her about their fight?

"Leon is scheduled to give his lecture next Friday evening at seven."

"Leon?" Zoë tried to process this information through her sluggish brain. "Oh, you mean the archaeologist guy."

"Should be interesting." Linda tucked a blanket securely around Ben's shoulders.

"Next Friday is Sarah and Mike's anniversary. They're having a party at The Tempest." She shuffled through the stack of envelopes. "In fact," she said, handing Linda the envelope, "you're invited as well."

"Too bad it's on the same night," Linda said. She tucked the invitation in her pocket.

"I'll phone Abbey this afternoon and let her know." Zoë held up the stamped envelopes. "I have to go now. I promised Sarah I'd drop these in the mailbox."

Zoë jogged to the post office and dropped the letters in the mailbox. To keep from thinking, she concentrated on the sound of her running shoes as they hit the pavement. Out of breath, she sat down on a nearby wharf, her mind a mass of confusion. Taking a deep breath, she tried to put her whirling thoughts in order. As much as she tried to block out her mother's words, they were like dead fish floating to the surface of her mind.

At ten minutes past eight, she rang her grandfather's doorbell. She didn't even know if he was home; some weekends he stayed in Corner Brook.

Opa opened the door, wearing his bathrobe. "Well, you're an early bird," he said, raising an eyebrow. "Come in, my dear." He held open the screen door.

Zoë followed him down the hallway to the kitchen.

Opa pulled out a chair at the kitchen table and gestured for her to sit. He poured a cup of tea from a pot on the back burner, put it in front of her, and took a seat at the table across from her. "What brings you this way so early in the morning?"

Zoë shrugged. "I woke up early, decided to go for a walk."

"Well, it's good to see you. Actually, I was going to call you. I talked with Oma on the phone last night and there's something we need to discuss." He picked up a muffin from a basket and offered it to her.

"No thanks."

He was about to put it down, changed his mind, and bit into it. "Your grandmother and I have decided to get back together," he said between bites.

"Will you be moving to Cape Prosper?"

"Actually, your grandmother will be moving here with me. The house at Cape Prosper needs work. The roof's been leaking, and we plan to have the place renovated. It will probably be late November or early December before we can move in.

"As you know," Opa continued. "We own a little piece of land off Cape Prosper. An island, really."

Zoë nodded. She had heard of the island, had seen pictures and paintings of the miniature lighthouse. The fact that she never actually saw it made it more mysterious.

"We always said we would give the island to our eldest grandchild." Opa peeled the paper lining from his muffin. "Of course, we thought that would be Erin. But then you came to us." He reached across the table and squeezed her hand. "Like an unexpected gift. You are very special to us, my dear."

Zoë choked back a sob. He had said *us*. Did Ans feel the same way about her?

"Anyway," Opa continued. "I called Sheila, my lawyer, and she's going to come by so we can sign papers to transfer the deed. We decided to let you have the island now."

Zoë stared at him, dumbfounded.

The phone rang and Opa got up to answer it.

They were going to give her an island, her very own island. Opa and Oma. Zoë's heart leapt with gladness. But just as quickly, she was plunged into despair. How could she accept their gift, knowing what she knew?

CHAPTER 16: Buried Secrets

"Sir, are you not my father?"
The Tempest

About two dozen chairs had been placed in the visitor's area of the museum, and when they filled up, more were brought in. Zoë sat between Linda and Abbey, waiting for everyone to be seated. Leon Morgan was already at the lectern. Zoë glanced at her watch. Seven-forty exactly. Mike and Sarah's party would be just getting started. When Sarah found out about the lecture, she urged Zoë to attend. Dr. Morgan was a respected colleague, she said. And besides, Zoë could always come to the party afterwards. Linda, of course, would also be late.

On the wall behind Dr. Morgan were colourful life-sized portraits of the Maritime Archaic Indians reconstructed by artists. There were also enlarged, grainy, black and white photographs of skeletons with knees drawn to their chests. From her research Zoë knew that archaeologists weren't sure if the group buried their dead that way because of some religious ritual or simply to save space.

After welcoming his audience and thanking them for coming out in such bad weather, Dr. Morgan got to the heart of his discussion. "The find here in Port au Choix is what we archaeologists like to refer to as 'a happy accident of preservation.'" He glanced behind him at the paintings and photographs. "The soil in this area is rich with calcium producing seashells, which have preserved bones that otherwise would have been destroyed."

More people came into the museum, and Dr. Morgan paused until they were seated. "The beach here is extremely alkaline," he continued. "Its excellent natural drainage accounts for the artifacts' extraordinary state of preservation.

"The meagre supply of tools and artifacts found at other sites gave a false representation that baffled scholars for years." Dr. Morgan's firm resonant voice filled the small room. "Sometimes, when information is faulty or when important pieces of information are missing, it is easy to come to the wrong conclusion. What we think we see is not always what's really there. But the find here in Port au Choix in the sixties has given us the puzzle's missing pieces. We are able to see these ancient people in a new light."

Zoë found it hard to concentrate. Dr. Morgan's words floated past her like pieces of wood drifting downstream. She glanced at Linda who was leaning forward, nodding and smiling. Abbey had brought along a spiral notebook to jot down comments.

"There can be value in examining the past," the professor was saying. "The past offers information that can help us change for a better future."

Zoë's mind kept slipping to her mother's diaries. The awful truth she had learned was always with her, a dark presence at the back of her mind. At times it was hard to grasp the horror of it. If the journals had remained in Aunt Caroline's basement, buried under boxes and piles of junk, she would never have excavated the truth. Her friend Omar, who had moved to Toronto from

Afghanistan, used to say: "The truth is like the sun. When it comes out, no one can hide from it." *Yes*, Zoë thought, thinking about what her mother had written. *A secret has a way of making itself known.*

The words written in her mother's elegant script were imprinted on Zoë's brain like an epigraph on a tombstone. No matter how hard she tried, she couldn't banish them from her memory. "I have killed my own child and stolen another."

Reenie wasn't her real mother. Zoë's life had been nothing more than an elaborate lie. She didn't know all the details, only that her biological mother—whom the journals referred to simply as M—died shortly after Zoë's birth. Reenie had met M at the maternity home and had moved into her apartment to take care of her when she got sick. M died shortly after Zoë was born, and Reenie claimed her as her own.

The audience erupted into applause, jolting Zoë out of her musings. The lecture was over, and people were getting out of their seats, moving toward the exit. A hand touched her shoulder, and she jumped.

"Sorry," Linda said, smiling. "But would you like a ride?"

"Um … I thought you had to go home first."

"I can drop you off before I go home," Linda said. "I've asked Josh to explain to Mike and Sarah that I will be a littler later than planned."

Zoë felt her heart sinking. She'd forgotten that Josh would be at the restaurant. She had not spoken to him since their fight.

Outside, people hurried to their cars, heads bowed against the wind and rain. Zoë climbed into the front seat with Linda. "Was it hard to get a babysitter?" She knew Linda depended a lot on Josh to look after the younger children.

"Madeline agreed to babysit."

"Madeline?"

"My little sister. She lives in St. Anthony but comes sometimes to visit on weekends." Linda turned onto the main street. "It's hard to believe that I once took care of *her*."

Zoë stared at her. "Madeline's your sister?"

Linda nodded. "Two months older than Josh, if you can believe it. My mother and I were pregnant at the same time."

Zoë was speechless. If Madeline was Linda's sister … that meant she was Josh's aunt. He hadn't lied to her. *How awful he must think I am to have accused him of lying.* She cringed, thinking of the last evening they had spent together.

Linda pulled into the parking lot at The Tempest. "Josh and Madeline are as close as brother and sister."

Zoë mumbled words of thanks, climbed out of the car, and ran for shelter.

A host dressed as a boatswain met her at the door. She told him she was with the van der Post party, and he ushered her through a wide set of doors into a large room filled with guests. Each table had a placard and a bouquet of flowers. A large banquet table laden with platters of food stood in the centre. Lobster, shrimp, and smoked oysters were nestled on beds of crushed ice. Various cheeses and meats were artfully arranged on porcelain platters. Waiters in leotards and pointed shoes carried silver trays of food, wine, and champagne around to the guests. Balloons and streamers hung from the ceiling, and a banner that read "Happy Anniversary Mike and Sarah" was strung along one wall.

Zoë scanned the room looking for Mike and Sarah and spotted them at a table near the window. Opa and Ans sat across from them. Next to Opa was an empty chair reserved for Zoë.

"Oh, look. Our granddaughter's here," Ans exclaimed.

Mike pulled out her chair. "You've missed Prospero," he said. "He was here a little while ago performing his magic." He pointed to the lavish banquet table where a group of guests were filling their plates. "He made all of that appear out of thin air."

"Came up from the floor," Ans said breathlessly.

"We only *thought* we saw it coming up from the floor," said Opa. "What the eye sees, the mind believes."

"In any case, it was quite remarkable," Ans said.

At that moment, three tall waitresses came over to their table, faces partially covered by black veils. Zoë knew from their costumes they were the goddesses Juno, Iris, and Ceres, characters in Shakespeare's *Tempest*. Iris leaned forward and kissed Sarah's cheek. "A contract of true love to celebrate."

Ceres gently laid her hand on Sarah's swollen belly. "May you be blessed with many more," she said in a high-pitched voice. Zoë thought there was something vaguely familiar about her.

"Can I get you something?" Iris asked her.

"A cup of tea," Zoë said.

"Let me get it," Ceres said. "Lots of milk, no sugar?"

Zoë nodded, wondering how she knew this.

Ceres was on her way to get the tea when Zoë saw Linda Carter and her husband Richard arrive. Ceres showed them to their table. From the way the Carters greeted her, it was obvious they knew her well. Zoë watched and listened as Ceres's high voice grew deep and familiar. "How's Auntie Maddie making out? Roger and Glenn got her drove crazy by now?"

Josh! She should have known. She glanced at the actors who were playing Iris and Juno and realized they too were guys.

A violin started playing, and Opa took Ans's hand and pulled her to her feet. They began waltzing cheek to cheek.

Josh returned with the tea, his voice again disguised. Through the black veil, Zoë could see his dark eyes dancing with merriment. She played along. "Thank you, oh Ceres, goddess of fertility." Although her voice was light, she was shaking inside. Josh carefully placed the tea on the table, giving a little bow before he departed.

Zoë's hands were shaking so badly, she could hardly hold her cup. Tea splashed onto the fancy tablecloth. She drank the hot soothing liquid, watching Josh out of the corner of her eye. He stopped to chat with guests, bringing wine, cups of tea, even a telephone directory for one man.

After a while, Iris came to the table balancing a tray of champagne flutes with one hand. Mike was at the banquet table, and Sarah was busy talking to some of the guests. Ans and Opa were still dancing. No one noticed when Zoë took a glass from the tray. Iris, who seemed occupied, didn't even ask her age. She'd never had champagne, and she coughed as it burned her throat. She sipped it slowly, savouring the smooth warmth that relaxed her stomach.

When her glass was empty, she looked around the room for Iris. He was standing by the banquet table talking with some of the guests. The tray of champagne flutes was on a table beside him. Zoë strolled over and picked up another glass.

The drink gave her a new confidence; the fear she had carried around all week had now vanished. However, no amount of champagne could make her forget the words in her mother's journal. "I have killed my own child and stolen another."

Zoë finished her drink and returned to her table. By now, she was starting to feel a little tipsy, and the room was tilting around her. Josh's mother was sitting at the table talking to Sarah. Mike and Ans were having a separate conversation at the end of the table. No one noticed when Zoë sat down. Sarah was showing Linda the latest pictures of Laura. "We couldn't have loved her more if I'd given birth to her myself."

"I'm not their child either," Zoë interrupted, the champagne giving her the courage to say what was on her mind.

Sarah stared at her, mouth gaping.

"I'm *not* Zoë," she charged, a little too loudly. Mike and Ans turned to look at her.

"Mum had an abortion." She hiccupped.

Mike cleared his throat and stared pointedly at Zoë.

"She killed your baby," she continued, unaware of Mike's reproving look.

"Oh, honey," Ans said, laying a hand on her arm.

Zoë glared at her. "Why would you care?"

Ans drew back her arm, a look of horror on her face.

"Zoë!" Mike said reproachfully. He peered at her closely. "You've been drinking, haven't you?"

"No!" Zoë said, her voice slurred.

"I'm taking you home." And before she could protest, Mike was gripping her arm, steering her toward the coat rack at the front of the room.

Just before she left the restaurant, she saw Josh standing by the cash register. She could only imagine the look on his face behind the black veil.

CHAPTER 17: Alone

"Why speaks my father so ungently?"
The Tempest

Zoë awoke with a pounding headache, her mouth dry. Bits and pieces of last night's conversations clung to the edge of her memory. Recollections, raw and shameful, crawled back into her consciousness. She recalled the look of horror on Sarah's face, Mike's rebuking frowns. And Josh—he saw and heard everything. Another memory that stirred in her mind was Ans's face creased with pain. She was clearly hurt.

Zoë got out of bed and pulled on jeans and a sweater. She went downstairs, uncertain about facing Mike and Sarah.

They were sitting at the dining room table talking, but fell silent when Zoë walked into the room. Mike looked down at his coffee mug. Sarah's back was stiff, her mouth grim. She gave Zoë a long, accusing stare but said nothing.

She took a seat at the long mahogany table, heart pounding. The silence was louder than any words.

Mike spoke first, his voice harsh. "You made quite a spectacle of yourself last night."

"I … I didn't mean," she faltered.

"Your antics upset everyone," Sarah said reproachfully. "Your grandmother especially."

Zoë hung her head.

There was a brief silence, and when Sarah spoke again, her voice was like acid. "What was that foolishness about your mother having an abortion?"

"I've been reading Mum's journals."

Sarah glared at her. "And she wrote that she aborted you?"

Zoë swallowed. Until now, she had not considered how much Sarah must resent her. How burdening it must have been for her to take Zoë into their home. She got up from the table, went upstairs, and returned moments later with her mother's journal. "It's all here," she said, tapping the page with her finger. Shreds of paper still clung to the spirals where pages had been ripped out.

"Let me see." Sarah took the journal and read aloud: "I have done a terrible thing. I have killed my own child and stolen another."

Mike's head jerked up.

Sarah gave Zoë a cold stare. "Is it true?"

She shrugged. "It's what Mum wrote."

"Oh the *selfish* woman." Sarah closed the journal and dropped it on the table.

Mike stood up, his face pale. "That can't be right," he said, reaching for the journal. "Why would Reenie write such things?"

"Caroline must have known the truth when she called here wanting to be rid of Zoë."

Mike gave Sarah a sharp look. "Caroline is no relation to Reenie. She might not have known."

Sarah's words were like blows. Zoë felt like a piece of lost luggage no one wanted to claim. What was going to happen to her now?

Sarah sat up straighter in her chair. "Daddy has always taught me to be honest," she said primly. "'Play by the rules, and you can't go wrong,'" he always said.

Zoë looked at the portrait of Charles. Steel grey eyes stared down at them from a thin narrow face. She took the journal from Mike and, without a word, left the room.

Behind her, Sarah's voice rose. "I wanted to call Hollis to arrange for paternal testing. That would have been the sensible thing to do."

"At the time, I had no doubt Zoë was my child." Mike's voice was low. "Besides, it may not be true. I can't imagine Reenie having an abortion."

Zoë hurried upstairs to her bedroom and closed the door. For a long time, she stared out the window, Sarah's cruel words echoing in her brain. Why hadn't she realized how Sarah felt about her? *Is it because I didn't want to?* she wondered. *Have I only seen what I wanted to see?* And although Mike was defending her, he had only ever been lukewarm toward her, not the loving father she'd hoped he would be. Certainly not the imaginary father she had conjured up as a lonely child. She had been clinging to an illusion. She could see now what should have been apparent from the start.

Through the closed door, she could hear Mike and Sarah's voices rising in anger. Zoë was grateful that Dora, who had taken Laura overnight, had not yet returned with her. To drown out the voices, she turned on her stereo.

Zoë spent the rest of the morning going through her mother's journals. She didn't go downstairs for lunch, and nobody came looking for her. She had not eaten since last evening and her stomach growled with hunger. But no way was she going downstairs to face Sarah.

She picked up the Polaroid picture and studied it. Rusty, JoJo, and Reenie. Could one of these women sitting beside Reenie be her birth mother? Perhaps Rusty was M. No doubt she got her name because of her red hair. The woman on the other side of Reenie had dark hair. Both women looked vaguely familiar, but Zoë couldn't place either of them. *What became of them?* she wondered. *Did Mum have contact with them after they left the home?*

She stayed in her room until mid afternoon, eating only a squashed chocolate bar she found in the drawer of her nightstand. Not once had Mike or Sarah come to see if she was okay. *I can't stay here*, she told herself. *Not where I'm not wanted.* From her drawer she took out a roll of bills, and counted out nearly a hundred dollars. Zoë had been saving the money she earned at the site. That, along with her allowance from Mike, made quite a nest egg. She stuffed the bills into the pocket of her jeans, got her backpack from her closet, and threw in a few items of clothing. She added the shoebox filled with her mother's paraphernalia. The bus that went to Corner Brook three times a week would be leaving in about an hour.

Zoë went to stand at the window. Although it was not quite four o'clock, it was already starting to get dark. The storm had gathered force, blowing dead, limp leaves around the street and driveways. The bare trees looked black against the darkened sky, and birds huddled together in tight little balls. Rain rolled down the window like tears. The houses on the street had the curtains drawn, and children and pets were safely inside. The street was deserted except for a child's red mitten writhing and twisting on the pavement. It looked so forlorn on the grey, wet concrete that Zoë had an urge to run outside and rescue it.

CHAPTER 18: A One-way Ticket

"Alas, the storm has come again."
The Tempest

Zoë walked the three kilometres to Annie's Garage and Take-out, which also served as the bus depot. Gusts of wind drove rain against her face. The storm had whipped the ocean into a mass of white foam. It felt good to be leaving, even if she didn't have a plan.

By the time she reached Annie's, Zoë had made up her mind to go to Opa's cottage. *He told me I could go there any time*, she reasoned. She would take the bus as far as Portland Creek then walk the two miles through the woods. She'd hole up in the cottage until she could figure out what to do.

It was nearly five thirty when the Viking Express, a converted school bus painted sky blue, drove into the parking lot. Zoë was just finishing her fish and chips. She wiped her hands on a napkin, threw the cardboard container in the garbage and followed the other passengers outside. The driver collected their fare as they got on the bus.

The bus smelled of wet wool and stale coffee. Zoë took a seat near the back and put her backpack under her seat. Pressing her face against the grimy window, she looked out at the gathering darkness. The wind blew empty chip bags, plastic bottles, and dead leaves around the parking lot.

The bus moved through the storm, wipers slapping the windows. By the time they passed Hawke's Bay, it was almost completely dark. Streetlights and lights from buildings all melted together. After a while, Zoë fell asleep and when she awoke, passengers were retrieving bags and suitcases. "Where are we?" she asked a woman in a green raincoat.

"Bellburns. Where's ye goin' to, my love?"

"Portland Creek."

"Next stop."

It was close to seven by the time the bus pulled into Judy's Diner and Variety store. Zoë went inside and bought a flashlight, potato chips, a carton of juice, packaged sandwiches, and muffins. She squeezed the items into her backpack and began the long trek through the woods in the darkness. The small flashlight didn't give off much light as she followed the narrow road, tripping over roots and large rocks. The walk seemed to take forever, and she wondered if she was on the right trail. Wind and rain beat against her face, and she stepped into large puddles of water.

By the time she reached the cottage, her clothes were soaked, her teeth clattering like castanets. She found the spare key that was kept in a flowerpot and opened the door. When she flicked the light switch, she realized there was no electricity. In the darkness, she stripped off her wet clothes and got a sweatshirt and a pair of flannel pyjamas from her backpack. Hastily, she got dressed and, still shivering, went to the kitchen drawer to get the candles that were kept there in case of an emergency.

Before long, Zoë had a fire roaring in the fireplace. She took the box containing Reenie's things from her backpack and spread the contents on the table. By the light of the candles, she sorted through cards, letters, and photographs, hoping to find something that might give her some clues about her birth mother.

Picking up a photograph, she saw herself as a trusting seven-year-old. Her legs and arms as thin as sticks, her hair uneven across the front where Reenie had cut it herself. There were pictures of Zoë as a smiling baby, a frowning toddler, pictures of Zoë and Reenie together. What would her fate have been if her mother … if Reenie had not stolen her? And if she was not Zoë Martin, then who was she?

Zoë continued to sort through the items, the flickering candles throwing leaping shadows on the cottage walls. In the fireplace, orange fists of flame curled around a piece of wood. Outside, the rain had stopped. The night was black and as still as a shadow. Zoë listened to the hoot of an owl and the faraway cry of a coyote.

After some time, she came across a small manila envelope. Dumping the contents onto the table, she discovered a medical health card, a social insurance number, and a library card. She had seen these items before but had paid little attention. Now as she examined them closely, she saw that the name on the cards was Madonna Josephine MacIsaac. There was a slip of paper with an address: 22 Beacon Street, Toronto. Why would Reenie have another woman's personal items? A thought struck her. Could the M in the journals be Madonna? It made perfect sense. If Madonna had died, Reenie would have kept her things.

Zoë carefully reread some of the earlier journals, searching for any other mention of M. She was so engrossed in her reading, she didn't hear the car when it pulled into the driveway. Its headlights made flares of light on the walls of the cottage. She glanced toward the window just as the driver turned off the engine. An intruder? Fear prickled her spine. Someone had broken into the cottage back in the summer. For all she knew, this person could be dangerous. Zoë looked around the room for a way to escape. Not knowing what else to do, she ran into the nearest bedroom. Trembling uncontrollably, she crawled into the closet.

With a pounding heart, she listened as the car door opened and slammed shut. If only there was a phone. Sarah often complained that there was no phone at the lake. But Opa had insisted he didn't want calls coming into the cottage.

Moments—but what seemed like hours—later, the door opened.

In the cramped space, Zoë wrapped her arms around her legs and pulled her head down to her knees.

Heavy footsteps walked across the wooden floor.

Zoë's heart was thumping like a drummer out of control.

The footsteps came closer.

She held her breath unable to move.

"Anybody home?"

Her heart began to beat faster.

"Anybody home?" the voice called again.

She felt herself go limp with relief. Josh! She got out of the closet and went to greet him.

"Mike asked me to come here to look for you," he explained.

"How did he know I was here?"

Josh grinned. "Nobody does anything around here without everybody knowing about it." He met her gaze. "Why are you here?"

Zoë was suddenly conscious of her dishevelled appearance. She saw herself as Josh must see her: baggy sweater and pyjama bottoms. Her hair was still wet and tangled into knots.

He picked up a photograph from the pile on the table. Zoë was about six, and her front teeth were missing.

"Cute," he said. He studied the photograph a moment before putting it back on the table. "There's a problem with Sarah," he said, becoming serious.

Zoë felt her heart speed up. She lowered herself onto the nearest chair. "The baby," she whispered. "Is there something wrong with Sarah's baby?"

Josh pulled up a chair and sat across from her. He reached across the table to cover her cold hand with his own. "Your father said there were complications. That's all I know."

Zoë felt a stab of guilt, remembering how she'd upset Sarah. Without meaning to, she burst into tears.

Josh let her cry, not saying anything. It was a couple of minutes before he spoke. "What's troubling you, Zoë? Why did you run away?"

She was about to deny running away, but instead blurted out the whole story. She started with the day Aunt Caroline came into her room to tell her about Mike. "I didn't know he existed," she said.

Josh listened without interrupting, letting her pour out her grief.

She told him about all the things she learned from her mother's journals. "I don't know where I belong anymore," she finished.

"That's terrible," Josh said, looking at her with concern. "But are you sure you got the facts straight?" He glanced at the cards, journals, and photographs spread on the table. "When we don't have all the facts, it's easy to jump to the wrong conclusion."

Zoë knew Josh was referring to her hasty conclusion that Madeline was his girlfriend. *This is different*, she told herself. *How many more facts do I need?* Still, she felt she should apologize to Josh for her behaviour. "Josh," she began. "I'm sorry I accused you of lying the night we went to Daniel's Harbour. I was wrong and I know that now."

"Don't worry about it," Josh said quietly.

Shivering, Zoë drew her arms around herself for warmth. Josh peeled off his coat and wrapped it around her shoulders. "It's late," he said quietly. "Why don't you gather your things, and I'll take you home?"

"Home?" Zoë felt a chill of loneliness. She didn't know where home was anymore.

"Actually, your dad said I should take you to your grandfather's," Josh said, as if reading her thoughts. "He said your grandfather doesn't want you staying here alone."

She was silent. Had Mike told Ans and Opa the news?

"They're worried about you," Josh continued.

Zoë stuffed her things back in her backpack. If Opa didn't want her here, she would leave. But what was to become of her? Would she end up living on the street, eating out of trash bins like some of the homeless people she'd seen in downtown Toronto?

It was past midnight when Josh pulled his car into Opa's driveway. Almost immediately the outside light came on, and Ans was standing in the doorway. She ushered them inside with barely a word of greeting. The displeasure on her face was obvious.

What were you thinking?" Opa demanded, his voice none too

gentle, his forehead knotted into a frown.

Ans laid a hand on his arm to silence him.

Zoë felt her heart sinking. Her grandfather had never been angry with her before.

Josh, who was standing in the doorway, coughed discretely.

"Thanks for all your help, young man," Opa said, acknowledging him for the first time.

"Glad I could help out, Sir."

Zoë remembered she was wearing his coat. She took it off and handed it to him.

Josh took the coat and laid his hand on her shoulder. "I'll drop by tomorrow to see you," he said before heading for the door.

Zoë turned to Ans. "What's wrong with Sarah? Josh says there are complications."

"Sarah's going to be fine."

"And the baby?"

"Your father will be by tomorrow. He'll explain everything."

Zoë could tell by the briskness of Ans's voice that she wasn't going to discuss it further. *Why should I even care?* she thought. But truth was she had been looking forward to this baby whom she thought would be her half brother or sister. That had been taken away from her now.

"I've made up the bed in the spare room," Ans said. "I think it's best that you go to bed now. You will stay with us until other arrangements can be made."

Other arrangements? They were already making arrangements. Would they send her to a foster home? A home for troubled teens? She had run away, after all. Broke into a cottage. Zoë walked slowly upstairs, her stomach tight with anxiety.

CHAPTER 19: A Time for Truth

"I will here shroud til the dregs of the storm be past."
The Tempest

Rubbing sleep from her eyes, Zoë looked around the small bedroom with the slanted ceiling. The only other furniture besides the bed was a small bureau, night table, and chair. The walls were bare except for a photograph of a middle-aged dwarf. He was sitting on a bed, wearing nothing but a hat, a towel draped around the lower half of his body. *Mexican Dwarf in his Motel Room in N.Y.C. 1970* was written at the bottom of the print. A Diane Arbus print, Zoë realized. She'd seen enough of her photographs to recognize them anywhere.

She got out of bed and got dressed, but instead of going downstairs, she sat on the bed, staring out the window at the grey morning. A light wind whistled through the bare trees and scattered dead leaves around the yard. How could everything have gone so bad in such a short time?

A rap on the bedroom door jolted her out of her musings. "Come in," she called.

Mike opened the door. He walked wearily across the room, his eyes hollow with fatigue, his face shadowed by a day-old beard.

"Mike?"

"Hello Zoë," he said. "How are you?" He sat down in the chair beside her bed.

"I'm fine," Zoë replied, mechanically. "How's Sarah?"

"Sarah's … home now."

"And the baby?"

He rubbed a hand over his unshaven face. "There *is* no baby, Zoë."

She slumped back against the wall. "Sarah lost the baby."

"It was a hysterical pregnancy. I've known for some time now."

Zoë had never heard of a hysterical pregnancy and imagined the fetus going all berserk inside the womb.

"There never was a baby," Mike explained. "Sarah wanted a child of her own so badly, she convinced herself she was pregnant. At first, even her obstetrician was fooled."

"You mean she was never pregnant?"

Mike nodded grimly.

"You must have known."

"Yeah." Mike laughed bitterly. "Her obstetrician thought it best if we didn't address the issue right away. But then later, she would not accept it. No one could convince her."

Zoë was quiet. She thought of Sarah's tummy filling out the fancy maternity clothes she was forever buying. She thought of the little white nursery across the hall from Mike and Sarah's bedroom. Hard to believe all those months there never was a baby.

Mike stood up. "I have to go now. I'll be in touch soon."

Zoë watched him walk away and felt a pang of sadness. He didn't say anything about her running away. He didn't say anything about taking her home.

Moments later, Opa entered the room carrying a tray of food. He seemed to be in a good mood, and there was no sign of the anger he'd shown the night before. "I've brought you something to eat," he said. "Your grandmother's famous chowder."

"Chowder? For breakfast?"

"It's ten past twelve." Opa placed the tray on the bed beside her. "I used to be a waiter at one time, you know."

"Really?"

"Well, not a good one. In fact, people used to call me the dumb waiter." Chuckling at his own lame joke, Opa poured a cup of tea from a little stainless steel teapot.

"You didn't have to do this, Opa. I could have gone downstairs."

"Thought you might like to be served in bed." He turned to meet Zoë's gaze, his face serious now. "I suppose your dad explained about Sarah."

"Yes," she said, her voice quiet.

"Shame that is. I can't understand why Mike let the charade go on so long."

"You knew about it?"

"Not until about a week ago."

Poor Sarah, Zoë thought.

"They were able to adopt a child," Opa said as if reading her thoughts. "I'm sure there will be more children for Sarah." He sat on the edge of Zoë's bed, peering at her closely. "It seems, my dear, it was around the time they found out about you that Sarah's imaginary pregnancy began."

She couldn't look at him. Was she responsible? Come to think of it, the pregnancy ended soon after Zoë showed Sarah Reenie's journal.

She fixed her eyes on the photograph of the Mexican dwarf.

"A Diane Arbus," Opa said, following her gaze.

"Kind of scary."

"That my dear, might not be attractive, but it really is a work of art." He reached out his hand to straighten the picture. "Arbus photographed a number of 'freaks' as she called them. She thought most people went through life fearing some kind of trauma. Freaks, according to Arbus, had survived their trauma. They had already passed their test in life. She saw them as aristocrats."

Zoë kept her eyes on the photograph. She knew most trauma was not as obvious as a physical deformity. She thought of her own hidden wounds. What was visible on the outside did not always match what was on the inside. And what about Sarah? Pregnant without a baby. What could be freakier than that?

Zoë felt her eyes fill with tears.

"What's wrong, love?" Opa took both her hands in hers, his face wrinkled with concern.

"Alexander, I wonder—" Ans stood in the doorway, taking in the scene. "Oh, my," she said. "What's wrong?" She pulled the chair closer to Zoë and sat down.

Her grandmother's voice held so much kindness that Zoë began to cry harder.

"Zoë. What is it? What's the matter?"

Between sobs, Zoë blurted out the story. She told them all the things she had learned from reading her mother's journals. "I'm not your grandchild," she finished.

During Zoë's emotional speech, Ans and Opa had remained silent. Now Zoë looked at them, waiting for a response. Opa's face was hard to read. Ans had turned pale.

There was an aching inside her that she had not felt since her mother's death. It mattered how her grandparents felt about her, and she'd obviously upset them.

Ans was the first to speak. "Oh, Zoë," she said. She got up from the chair and sat down on the bed beside her. "It doesn't matter what your mother wrote in her journals."

Before she had a chance to respond, Zoë found herself cradled against her grandmother's shoulder. She was aware of Ans rocking her, murmuring soothing words.

Opa went to stand by the window.

"The only thing that matters to us is you," Ans was saying. "It doesn't matter who you are or how you came to be. It's you we have grown to love."

"Poor Maureen," Opa said, turning away from the window. "I wish I had been more supportive. I feel we let her down badly."

Ans swallowed as if she was having difficulty getting the words out. "I should have paid more attention to what Reenie wanted. We drove her away." Turning to Zoë, she said, "I made a mistake. I am sorry for everything. I hope you can forgive me."

In response, Zoë buried her face in her grandmother's neck.

Opa turned to look out the window. Zoë followed his gaze. Tiny rays of light were trying to break through the thick dark clouds.

Ans squeezed Zoë's shoulder. "You are ours now. Nothing in the world can change that."

CHAPTER 20: Looking for Mum

"Thy mother was a piece of virtue,
and she said thou wast my daughter."
The Tempest

"Zoë?"

"Huh."

Josh put his hand on her shoulder. "Zoë, you're miles away. Everything okay?"

Zoë nodded. She'd been at Opa's house for a whole week now. Josh had come by to visit as promised. "I was thinking about my relatives."

"Ans and Alexander?"

"I was thinking about my mother—my birth mother." Zoë glanced at the small table where Reenie's journals and other personal items were spread out. She told Josh about finding the envelope with Madonna MacIsaac's library card and social insurance number. "In the journals, Mum—Reenie —refers to my birth mother as M. I think it might be Madonna." She picked up the Polaroid and showed it to Josh. "I believe Madonna's the woman with the red hair. They called her Rusty."

Josh studied the picture carefully. "If I had to bet on any of these women being your mother, I would put my money on this one." He pointed to the dark-haired woman. "Same face and eyes as yours."

Zoë took the picture from him and looked intently at the woman. *Josh is right*, she thought. Funny she hadn't seen the resemblance when it was right in front of her. And then it struck her. "Madonna Josephine. JoJo! Of course." Why hadn't that occurred to her before?

Josh looked at Zoë. "Are you going to try to find her?"

Zoë shook her head. "She's dead. But I'm hoping to find out who she was."

"Anything I can do to help?"

She handed him one of the journals. "You can go through this; take note wherever Reenie refers to M."

"Sure, I can do that," Josh said. For the next while, he combed through the journals while Zoë scrutinized the items on the table, hoping to find anything else she might have missed.

"Here's something interesting," Josh said after reading halfway through the first journal. He began to read: "Rusty had her baby, a little boy she named Paul Richard. He was born with a serious heart defect and is not expected to live. Rusty is devastated. My heart aches for her."

"So sad," Zoë said. "But at least we now know that the red-haired woman is not my birth mother."

Josh went back to his reading, and Zoë picked up a journal from the table. She had been reading for only a few minutes when she came across an entry that aroused her interest: "Betsy has invited me to her parents' cottage for the weekend. They live in

Wolfville, and the cottage is nearby." Zoë flipped through the pages looking for more information and found an entry written a few days later: "We had so much fun at the lake. Mr. and Mrs. Wheaton are both so kind."

"Betsy Wheaton," Zoë said aloud.

Josh glanced up at her.

"I found a name," Zoë explained, "and I'm going to phone every Wheaton in Wolfville, Nova Scotia, until I find Betsy."

Zoë dialled directory assistance. The operator told her there were thirteen Wheatons listed. "Do you have a first name or an address?" she asked.

"Can you give me *all* the numbers?"

"I'm sorry," she said. "I am unable to do that. Please call back when you have more information." Before Zoë could say another word, there was a sharp click.

"Uncle Mark," she said.

"Who?" Josh gave her a puzzled look.

"Uncle Mark works at the public library in Halifax. Maybe he can help me find the numbers." Zoë looked at her watch. "I'm expected at the site in half an hour," she said. "After work, the team is having a little get together at someone's house. Sort of a goodbye party. I don't have much time."

Zoë picked up the telephone. Less than five minutes later, she had the numbers she needed.

Out of the first six calls, she got three answering machines, a busy signal, and two wrong numbers. On the seventh attempt, the phone was answered almost immediately. The voice on the other end was friendly, putting her at ease. "I'm looking for a Betsy Wheaton," Zoë said.

"That would be my daughter. Betsy McPherson she is now. Lives in Prince Edward Island with her family. They own a farm there."

"Betsy was a friend of my mother's," Zoë explained. "Mum died some months ago."

The woman clucked with sympathy. "Hold on, dear, while I find the number."

Moments later, she was back on the line. She gave the number to Zoë who jotted it down. "Betsy's home most days, so it shouldn't be hard to reach her."

"Thank you."

"You take care, dear," the woman said before hanging up.

With shaking hands, Zoë dialled the number. The phone rang five times and she was about to hang up when someone answered. It sounded like a teenage boy. She wondered if he was born while his mother was at the maternity home. Not likely, she told herself. Most of the babies born at the home were given up for adoption.

"Would Betsy Wheaton … uh … Betsy McPherson be in?"

"Mommm!"

After what seemed like a long time, a woman came to the phone. "Hello?"

"Betsy McPherson?"

"Yes."

"I'm Zoë Martin. I believe you knew my mum, Reenie Martin."

There was a sharp intake of breath, followed by a long silence. In the background Zoe could hear a television, running water. "Hello?" she said, wondering if the woman was still there.

"Reenie Martin's little girl." The woman's voice was muffled, as if she was crying.

"I was hoping you could give me some information on one of Mum's friends."

"So Reenie got the little girl she wanted. I often think of her. She came to the Home of the Guardian Angel shortly after I did. I wish now I had kept in contact. Your mother was a comfort to me in the last days of my pregnancy." There was a deep intake of breath. "She had your name picked out long before you were born. Picked it out of a baby book. It means life."

A sharp pain twisted Zoë's stomach. How hard it must have been for Reenie to have an abortion. No wonder she took another woman's baby when she saw the opportunity.

"Well, well," the woman continued. "How is she?"

Zoë swallowed. "She died some months back."

"Oh my dear, I'm so sorry. I ... I didn't know."

"Do you remember a woman named Madonna who was also at the home? I think she was called JoJo."

"No dear, I don't remember anyone by that name."

Zoe swallowed back her disappointment. Was this going to be a dead end? "There was another woman. Rusty," she said. "Do you remember her?"

"Rusty ... That would be Susan. Beautiful woman, she was. They called her Rusty because of her long, gorgeous red hair. But it's been so long. I'm afraid I wouldn't know how to get in touch with her. Don't even remember her last name. Probably wouldn't recognize her if I passed her on the street."

Zoë didn't know what else to say.

"Sorry I'm not able to be of much help," Betsy said.

"Thank you for your information," Zoë said.

"Good to hear from you, dear. You take care now," Betsy said, then hung up.

Zoë struggled to hold back the tears that were burning behind her eyelids. The conversation had upset her more than she expected.

Josh put down the journal he'd been reading and looked at her expectantly.

Zoë shook her head. "The only thing I learned is that Rusty's real name is Susan." She picked up the Polaroid from the table and studied it.

"I'm sorry," Josh said.

"Oh my God!" Zoë gasped, the realization slamming into her like a tidal wave.

"What is it?" Josh asked, rushing to her side.

"Susan," she said, her voice almost a whisper. "Rusty is Suzie Q."

CHAPTER 21: Pay Dirt

"I prithee remember I have done thee worthy service."
The Tempest

The dig had been cancelled the day of the storm, so it had been two weeks since Zoë was at the site. She was at one end of the trench, Jessie at the other. They had been digging for two hours now, and Zoë's back and shoulders ached. She welcomed the pain, however. It helped take her mind off all the rotten things that were happening in her life. *It's good to be back*, she thought. She was looking forward to the gathering this afternoon at Monty's house.

Zoë had noticed a lack of enthusiasm among the team. They certainly didn't have the passion they once had. *They're discouraged*, she realized. She knew Patty, especially, was disappointed. After digging more than fifty trenches, they had not accomplished what they'd set out to do. A lot of money and resources had been spent, and they didn't know if they were even digging in the right place. Still, Zoë was happy to have had the opportunity to work here. She had made a number of friends, and she had learned a lot about the prehistoric people who had lived here thousands of years ago. The hands-on experience had taught her more than any textbook on archaeology ever could.

"Time for a break," Monty called. The team took their breaks and lunch at the same time every day. For some reason, they seemed to think that was important.

Zoë climbed out of her pit and went to get her backpack. Since she'd been staying with Oma and Opa, she had been packing her own lunches. She pulled out a small container of pineapple juice and a banana. She spread her jacket on the ground and sat on it.

Abbey came to sit beside her. "Are you okay, Zoë?" She peered at her with concern. "You seem … I don't know … quiet."

As much as she wanted to unburden herself, Zoë felt she couldn't tell Abbey about what had been happening in her life. "I'm just tired," she said, forcing a reassuring smile. Truth was, she was still reeling from the shock of her conversation with Betsy. Reenie never once mentioned that Suzie was at the maternity home or that she had lost a baby. No wonder the poor woman was in and out of the mental hospital. Suzie must have moved to Ontario when Reenie did. *So many secrets*, she thought. *So many lies.*

"How is Sarah doing? She must be devastated about losing her baby."

Sarah's pregnancy. Another lie. "Sarah's fine," Zoë said vaguely. She had not seen Sarah since she left the house on that stormy afternoon. Mike had called a couple of days ago to invite her to Laura's birthday party. She would go, she decided. No matter what happened, she would always think of Laura as her little sister. Zoë sighed. It wasn't going to be easy facing Sarah again.

After the break, the team moved half-heartedly back into the trenches. They looked exhausted, Zoë thought.

Zoë had been digging for about twenty minutes when she felt her trowel hit something hard. *A rock*, she thought, but she carefully brushed away the earth from around it. After a few minutes, a stone object appeared, about six inches in length. "I found something," she told Jessie.

Jessie came to squat beside her. "Careful," she said, as Zoë dug around the object with her trowel. When it was completely exposed, she picked it up.

"Oh my God!" Jessie shrieked.

"What is it?"

"Oh my God, Zoë. It's a gouge! Monty!" she called. "Come see!"

Monty appeared almost immediately. "Look! A gouge!" Jessie said, excitedly.

Monty accepted it gingerly. He turned it around and around in his hands, a stunned look on his face. "Where did you get this?" he asked.

"Zoë found it in our pit."

"Hey guys!" Monty called. "You gotta come see this!"

The team began emerging from their pits.

"What is it?" someone asked.

Monty held out the gouge. There were excited shouts all around.

"Yes!" Abbey said, punching her fist in the air.

Zoë and Jessie climbed out of the pit. By now, everyone had gathered around Monty.

"I can't wait for Patty to see this," Monty said. "She's going to be so happy. Where is she, by the way?"

"I think she's down at Phillip's Garden," someone said.

"Tim." Monty looked at one of the team members. "Would you go fetch her? She'll want to know about this."

"Sure," Tim said. He laid down his trowel.

"Oh, she's going to be so happy," Abbey said. "I can't wait to see her face."

Tim was walking away when Jimmy, the practical joker, said, "Wait. Wait. I have an idea." He looked around at the team. "Why don't we wrap up the gouge and give it to Patty as a sort of going away present."

Monty looked skeptical.

"I love it. I love it," Jessie said. "She's going to flip out."

"Great idea," someone else said.

Monty pulled some bills from his pocket and handed them to Tim. "I guess we can hold off telling Patty the big news for a couple of hours. Go down to the drugstore and buy some wrapping paper."

By now, everyone was out of the trenches, standing around talking excitedly. "I knew we'd find something," one of the members said.

"Yes," someone else agreed. "I knew it would only be a matter of time."

Zoë spotted Jake, who had come out on his porch. She waved.

"Jake," Jessie called. "Come down here."

Jake came down the path wearing bedroom slippers. "What's goin' on?" he asked as he approached them.

"We found a gouge," Monty said.

"G'wan," Jake said. "Where'd ye find it?"

"Zoë found it, actually. It was in her trench."

Jake turned to Zoë. "Oh, my dear, Patty's gonna be some glad to hear that."

Zoë felt a surge of pride. She knew archaeology was teamwork, and all the members had contributed to finding the gouge. Still, she was the one who had actually unearthed it.

"Patty told me more than once how she'd love to find a gouge," Jake continued. "It would be proof, she said, that the Maritime Archaic Indians had their habitation site on my land." He shook his head. "God bless the dear woman."

"Coming to the party this afternoon?" Monty asked.

"Lookin' forward to it," Jake replied. "I was just whipping up some coconut squares."

Although Jake had offered to give them a ride, Zoë, Jessie, and Abbey decided to walk the two kilometre to Monty's house. Zoë was so keyed up, she needed to walk off her energy. Her heart pounded with excitement. She had found a valuable artifact, one that would provide important information about the life of the Maritime Archaic Indians.

"It's that house over there," Abbey said, after they had walked to the other end of Port au Choix. She pointed to a saltbox with peeling white paint that faced the ocean.

Most of the team had already arrived. They were in the living room standing around a table laden with sandwiches, cookies, and squares. Bottles of soda had been put out along with a bowl of punch.

"Hi you guys," Patty greeted them. "I'm so glad you could come." She had changed out of her working clothes and was wearing black pants and high-collared white blouse.

"Wouldn't have missed it for anything," Abbey said.

Zoë poured herself a glass of soda. She was too excited to eat anything.

The team was in high spirits, laughing and joking. It was difficult to believe they had been so gloomy just hours earlier. Monty couldn't stop smiling.

About an hour after they arrived, Patty stood. "I'm happy so many of you could make it," she said, looking around the room. "You have been a great team and I'm proud of you. Some of you will be returning next season, but this will be the last time this group will be together as a team. We may not have accomplished everything we set out to do, but we will be back. The work here is very important and it will go on."

"Thanks, Patty," Monty said, moving toward her with the wrapped gift in his hand. "You have been an inspiration to us all. On behalf of the team we got you a little thank you gift."

"Oh that's so nice," Patty said, accepting the gift. "It's heavy. Feels like a paperweight."

"Well I suppose it could be used as a paperweight." Monty winked slyly, as the room erupted into laughter.

"Why don't you open it and find out?" Jake urged. "Yeh never knows what it might be til yeh opens it."

There were murmurs of agreement around the room.

Nodding, Patty tore off the outside wrapping and removed the layers of tissue paper.

"A gouge?" Patty's eyes went wide with disbelief. "Where did this come from?"

"It was in Zoë's pit," Monty said. "She found it this afternoon."

Then everyone was talking at once.

Patty let out a whoop. "I can't believe it! You guys are really something." Tears glittered in her eyes. "You guys are really something else."

CHAPTER 22: An Apology

"But, O, how oddly will it sound, that I
must ask my child forgiveness."
The Tempest

"Looks like quite the party," Opa said as they drove into Mike and Sarah's driveway.

Zoë nodded, taking in the colourful balloons tied to the veranda. A large banner with "Happy Birthday Laura" was hung across the window. Cartoon characters stood on the front lawn with signs announcing that Laura had turned two years old today.

Zoë's stomach fluttered with nervousness. It was her first visit at Mike and Sarah's house since she left two weeks ago. Mike had called her a couple of times. He told her in one conversation that she was welcome to come back and live with them. Zoë couldn't imagine living here knowing how Sarah felt about her.

"Are you okay?" Opa asked as they approached the veranda.

Zoë forced a smile. "Yeah," she said. With trembling hands, she rang the doorbell.

Sarah opened the door. "Zoë? Alexander?" She stepped aside to let them in. "We were wondering where you were."

"Hi, Sarah," Zoë said, stepping into the foyer.

"I'm glad you could come." Sarah led them into the living room where bright streamers hung from the ceiling. Balloons bobbed from chandeliers and from the handrail on the stairs.

"I see you've been working hard as usual," Opa said.

Sarah gave him a thin smile. She looked pale and she had obviously lost weight.

"Where's the birthday girl?" Opa asked.

As if on cue, Laura toddled into the room, moving stiffly in a fancy party dress, a pink satin gown with lace on the sleeves and collar. She had a teddy bear painted on her chubby cheek. "Opa," she cried happily.

"There's my party girl." Opa swept her off her feet and lifted her into the air.

Zoë blinked back tears. She had missed little Laura.

Opa put Laura down, and Zoë gave her a hug. "Laura," she said, "did you have a lot of friends at your party?"

Laura nodded. "Eleventeen." She held up four chubby fingers.

"There's still a lot of kids downstairs in the rec room," Sarah said. "Prospero the magician is here. Josh brought his brothers over." She glanced at the clock on the wall. "The adults should be arriving shortly."

Laura tugged on Zoë's hand. "Down tairs," she said.

"You want me to go downstairs?"

Afraid Laura would trip in her fancy dress, Zoë carried her to down the steps to a large rectangular room. About half a dozen kids were gathered around Prospero the magician. Many of them had flowers, balloons, and teddy bears painted on their faces. She watched a loonie magically appear in the magician's hand from out of a child's ear. There was loud cheering and clapping. "Do it again," the child pleaded.

"That's enough magic for today," Prospero said, taking a bow.

Josh was sitting at the far end of the room wearing a paper party hat. One of his brothers sat on his knee. Zoë walked across the room and sat beside them. Laura wandered off to where some little kids were playing.

"You missed Happy the clown," he said. "You could have had your face painted."

"Oh, no!" she said, feigning disappointment.

While they were talking, the magician came to sit across from them on a small sofa. "Whew," he said. "I think I've used up all my magic."

Josh introduced him as Henry Gammon from Saint John, New Brunswick. "Henry's been doing magic shows since he left high school."

"My grandmother was impressed by how you made a banquet table appear out of thin air," Zoë said. "How did you do that?"

"Misdirection," he explained. "The trick is to create an illusion, to make people see things that are not really there."

"Sounds complicated."

He shrugged. "It's easier than you think. Usually, people are so focused on the activity they miss the obvious." He smiled. "Sometimes they can't see what is right in front of them."

"How did you get interested in magic?" Josh asked.

Henry told them about meeting the Great Kristen who came to New Brunswick when Henry was seven years old. "I knew then what my future would be," he said.

Josh glanced at his watch. "I better get the kids home," he said. "Glenn," he called to his brother, who was playing with a train set. "Time to go." He turned to Zoë. "Maybe we could go out sometime soon."

"I'd like that," she said, relieved that Josh still wanted to go out. Although he'd been to visit her at Opa's, she was afraid he wouldn't ask her out again after their last disastrous date.

"I should be going too." Henry got up from the sofa. "It was nice meeting you, Zoë. And I'll see *you* at work, Josh."

After the last child was collected, Zoë took Laura upstairs. She found Mike in the kitchen arranging hors d'oeuvres on a platter. The counter was lined with bottles of wine, various cheeses, cold cuts, and boxes of crackers. He squeezed her shoulder. "It's good to see you, Zoë."

"I'm glad to be here. Laura is really growing."

"Yes, I can't believe she's two already." Mike reached out to finger the delicate cross on her neck. "That's a lovely necklace, Zoë."

"It's the one Oma gave me for my birthday."

"We have good news," Mike said. "We may be able to adopt another baby within a year."

"That's great! A girl or boy?"

"We would like a boy, but we don't want to cut our chances in half."

Zoë nodded.

Mike put his hand on her arm. "And how are you doing, Zoë?"

"Me? I'm fine."

"Getting on okay with Oma and Opa?"

"We get along great."

Mike was silent for a moment. "I feel I should apologize for everything you had to go through. It must have been very difficult."

Zoë merely nodded.

"If I'd faced my responsibilities," Mike continued, "you wouldn't have found yourself in the situation you're in. I hope you are able to forgive me."

"It's okay," she said, reaching out and touching his arm.

CHAPTER 23: Finding Mum

"We are merely cheated out of our lives."
The Tempest

Zoë awoke around midnight, her thoughts racing. Ever since her phone call to Betsy, she'd had a nagging sense that something was not right. Turning on the light, she sat up in bed. The journals were stacked neatly on the bureau in random order. There were gaps in time; weeks, months, and even years were missing. How could they be relied upon to tell an accurate story?

Zoë picked up the Polaroid from her night table, Betsy's words ringing in her ears. *Your mother was a comfort to me in the last days of my pregnancy.* Reenie came to the maternity home shortly after Betsy did. If she'd had an abortion, why would she still be there in the last days of Betsy's pregnancy? And why wouldn't Betsy remember JoJo? All three of the women in the photograph had flat stomachs. The photo was obviously taken early in their pregnancies, before they started to grow. Their babies must have been due around the same time. Surely JoJo would have been at the home while Betsy was there. *People miss the obvious*, Prospero had said. Zoë stared hard at the picture. Maybe the truth had been in front of her all the time and she hadn't realized it.

She carefully studied the woman with the dark hair. She knew now where she'd seen her before. Her heart quickened. Slipping quietly out of bed, she pulled on her robe, her hands shaking so badly she could barely tie the belt.

Downstairs, Ans and Opa were watching the news. "Can't you sleep, love?" Ans asked, looking away from the small television.

Zoë scanned the pictures on the wall. Someone had moved the portrait she was looking for. It was now next to Diane Arbus's *A Lobby in a Building*. Zoë compared the painting with the photograph in her hand. There was no mistake about it. The woman in the portrait and the woman in the photograph were the same. But why would Opa have a picture of JoJo?

Opa stood up, yawned. "Time for bed. Early meeting tomorrow."

"Opa," Zoë said. "Who is that woman in the painting?"

"Which painting?"

"That one next to *A Lobby in a Building*."

"This?" Opa touched the painting. He gave Zoë a perplexed look. "Why, it's Maureen," he said. "Your mother. Don't you recognize her?"

"It was done by my cousin," Ans said, coming to stand beside them. "Daniel Piet. I don't know if you've heard of him. He has gained some fame."

Zoë suddenly felt light-headed. The painting blurred in front of her. The realization was like a fist to the stomach. A ragged sob escaped her throat, and she could feel her legs buckling. Making her way to the nearest chair, she put her head down to her knees. *Oh, dear God, it's Maureen … my mother.*

"Are you okay, Zoë?" Opa's voice was filled with concern.

"She's as white as a ghost," Ans exclaimed, rushing to her side. "What is it that's upsetting you?"

"That's ... *not* my mother," Zoë said, feeling strangely detached.

Ans and Opa were both looking at her oddly.

"She's not my mother," Zoë repeated. "Well ... not the woman I lived with."

Ans looked confused. "I don't understand, dear."

Zoë struggled to find words to make them see the truth. She pointed to the photograph in her hand. "*This* is Reenie..."

Ans took the picture and looked at it, a puzzled frown on her face.

Zoë gestured to the painting on the wall. "That is *not* the woman who raised me."

Ans continued to stare at her.

Zoë told her about reading the journals. She explained about finding the social insurance number and other personal items belonging to Madonna Josephine—JoJo.

"It all makes sense now," she said. "The journals belonged to more than one person. Mum, that is, Reenie wrote the early ones. JoJo must have written the later accounts."

Ans and Opa were staring at her. "Dear God, Zoë," Ans said. "Are you telling us that your mother died years ago? That you were raised by ... by an impostor?"

Zoë nodded. "The woman who raised me was Madonna Josephine MacIsaac. JoJo.

After Reenie died, JoJo not only took me, she took Reenie's identity." It totally made sense now. The M referred to in the journals was Maureen, not Madonna as Zoë first thought.

"Good lord in heaven," Opa said.

Oma continued to stare at her, a look of horror on her face.

Zoë understood now why JoJo/Reenie never wanted her to meet Mike and his family. And no wonder poor Suzie was so concerned about who was going to take care of Zoë after Reenie died. In Suzie's confused mind, Zoë was still the infant JoJo had stolen. Zoë recalled the time Suzie was convinced Reenie was dead. And then there was the time she called Mum ... called JoJo by her real name. It was clear now why JoJo stopped going to see her at the hospital. She was afraid Suzie would let the cat out of the bag.

Zoë went to stand by the window and looked out at the dark night. "JoJo was the 'friend' who called Mike to tell him Reenie had had a miscarriage," she said. She turned to face Ans. "How can you live with someone your whole life and not know who they are? How could she do that to me?"

"What do I do now?" Zoë asked. They were sitting around the table having tea. It was well after midnight, but no one was eager to go to bed.

"The first thing you have to do is forgive her," Ans said.

"Forgive her?" Zoë echoed.

"The answer always lies in forgiveness, my dear," Opa said.

"But she lied to me. Kept me from seeing you. My life could have been so different."

"Was it all bad? Your life?"

Zoë thought of all the good times she'd had with JoJo. She had loved Zoë, and despite everything, she had been happy.

"We celebrate the life we are given, not the one we hope to have," Opa said quietly. "I know you must feel terribly betrayed." He reached across the table and squeezed her hand. "But if you don't cut the strings of resentment and make peace with this, it will destroy you."

"But JoJo wasn't my mother," Zoë said, bitterness leaking into her voice. "She lied to me."

Ans was staring straight ahead with a faraway look on her face. "I feel I have played a part in this, too," she said. "I have to share the blame as much as anyone." She put down her cup, her gaze meeting Zoë's. "But I must forgive myself. Alexander is right. If you do not want to be bound to this hurt forever, you must find some way to forgive her."

Forgive? This was something Zoë would have to think about. She was struck with a new thought. "I am your grandchild, after all," she said. "Mike really *is* my dad." And as devastated as she was about JoJo's deceptions, it was comforting to know that her real mother had not lied.

Ans reached for her hand. "My dear, that's the last thing we're concerned about. We accepted you as ours from the moment you came into our lives."

EPILOGUE

"What's past is prologue."
The Tempest

December 1, 1997

Dear Amber:

I am so excited about my visit. Imagine, our whole Christmas vacation together! I can't wait to see you again.

I will be going to school in Corner Brook next term. I will be living there with my grandparents. Living with my father and his wife did not work out. I will tell you more about it when I see you. In fact, I have a lot of things to tell you.

I feel sad about leaving Port au Choix. As you know, I have grown to love the place. But my grandparents have a house not far from here. We will be returning every weekend. Josh is starting his first year at Sir Wilfred Grenfell College in Corner Brook in September, so I will have at least one friend there. Another good thing is that the school in Corner Brook has an art program. Opa and Oma are encouraging me to "nurture my talent," as Oma puts it.

I am glad that Suzie Q is doing well and that Aunt Caroline is helping her.

See you in a couple of weeks.

Love, Zoë